7

Fri

to another!

BETWEEN THE PANELS

(A GEEKY LOVE STORY)

KAI KIRIYAMA

xoxo
Kai Kiriy '16

To Gail Simone.
None of this would have happened if it hadn't been for you.

CHAPTER ONE

The door opened with the familiar "bing bong" of the doorbell, letting the staff inside the shop know that someone had come in. A smile tugged at the corners of her lips, she hadn't been to the shop for a little more than a year, and her comic reading habits waned whenever she got bored, or fell too far behind with the current continuity of the big-two publishers.

She was dressed in a black skirt and top, black leggings, and running shoes. Her shoulder length hair, dyed a reddish-purple, hung loose around her face and she adjusted her glasses before tucking an annoying strand of her hair behind her ear. She had roundish features, and a button nose that she thought was far too cookie-cutter, and she thought the combination made her look far more immature than she felt. She was a bit on the short side, average was more apt, but she always wished she was taller, and she had thighs that had been blessed by the god of thunder himself.

She sighed happily as she entered the store, the comforting smell of paper and ink filling her nose as she made her way from the foyer into the store proper. The shop was one of the ones where people ignored you for the most part. She'd never made any friends coming to this place, and she was happy with that. It was a store that served a purpose but didn't foster a tight-knit community. She'd never been harassed for being a geek girl; she'd never had to prove her geekiness to random strangers. It was quiet when she went, usually, unless she showed up on a Wednesday afternoon when all the new issues were released. Then she tried to avoid the store, because it was busy and she didn't want to cope with crowds of people in the already over-filled space. She didn't even stop to look at the free preview magazines lining the long table in the entrance, she was on a mission and she wasn't about to let herself get distracted.

It had been a while, but she remembered the store well enough. She slipped her messenger bag off her shoulder and set it on the floor next to the till without thinking.

"Hey, how's it going?"

She was totally pulled out of her own thoughts as the young man behind the counter greeted her. She looked up to see who had spoken and paused. He was tall and slender, with dark, longish hair slicked back, brown eyes, pale skin, and narrow features. He had a sharp nose and cheekbones that would make any fan of British television detectives swoon. He was dressed in a plaid buttoned shirt with a grey sweater overtop.

Oh shit, he's really cute.

She flashed him a coy smile. "Hey yourself."

He grinned widely in return. "You look kind of lost."

"I, uh… I haven't been in here for a while," she admitted, peering around the store, taking off her jacket and draping it over her arm. "Um…"

"What are you looking for?" he asked.

"I don't know, exactly," she replied. "I'm going to go get a bunch of stuff signed at the expo in a couple weeks and I guess I'm looking for back issues? They're still in the same place, right?"

He nodded his head toward the corner of the store behind and to the opposite side of the till. "Yeah, they're all still there."

"Oh, good," she replied. "I guess I'll figure out what my friends want me to get signed for them then."

"Good luck, feel free to ask if you need any help."

"I'm pretty sure that I can figure out the alphabet," she teased.

"I'm sure you can, but not everyone else is as clever."

She shook her head. "I sure as hell don't miss working retail."

He laughed in response and waved her off to go and look at the back issues. She didn't say anything as she made her way across the store. The back issue shelves were massive, the lower shelves pulled out as drawers, and it all was alphabetized, just like she'd expected. She pulled her phone out of her pocket as she flipped through the titles, looking for series and issues from the creator who she was planning to go and meet and have sign comics. She snapped a few pictures of the issues she found, sending the pictures of the cover art to out of town friends, asking which covers they would prefer.

While she waited for responses, she continued browsing the titles, looking for more by her idol. Checking her phone every time it buzzed and picking out the comics that her friends had asked to have signed. She didn't notice when he walked up behind her.

"You finding everything okay so far?"

She jumped, startled, and nearly dropped her phone and the pile of comics in her hands. "Holy shit," she muttered.

His face lit up in a bright smile and he started to laugh. "I'm sorry."

"No you're not," she replied, regaining her composure. "Not yet, anyway."

"You'd think I'd have heard that kind of threat already, but I'm pretty sure that's a new one."

"You get a lot of threats?" she asked.

7

"Sometimes," he replied. "Depends on the day and how much of an ass I'm being."

"Well, you're not being too much of an ass," she assured him, rebalancing all of the things in her arms. "I'm just jumpier than I'd realized. So I suppose you're forgiven."

"That's a relief, I didn't want to have to fight you."

"We'll take that outside," she joked. "Wouldn't wanna ruin the merchandise."

"I'm gonna have to use the buddy system to get home tonight, aren't I?"

She snorted. "I could be your buddy."

"That would defeat the purpose, wouldn't it?"

She shrugged in response, grinning widely. It had been quite a while since she'd met anyone willing to banter back and forth with her as quickly and easily as this boy had. It was pleasant, and she appreciated his sense of humor. It matched hers, and she wished she'd had something else clever to say.

"So, uh, are you finding everything all right so far?" He looked past her where she'd pulled out a single drawer and had six issues spread out on top of the bagged and boarded back issues within. She caught his glance beyond her and turned slightly, taking a better look at the mess she'd made.

"I'm waiting to get messages back from my friends," she said, waggling her phone. "I don't know which ones they want me to get signed for them."

"You must really like your friends," he replied.

"Not really," she teased. "I'm just too nice for my own good. Besides, it's not like it's every day that you get to meet the comic creator who unintentionally introduced you to the majority of your circle of friends, right? Gotta take full advantage of the opportunity and make sure that I now have leverage over said friends."

"So it's emotional blackmail?" he suggested.

"Less emotional blackmail, more like straight up hostage taking. I now get to negotiate favors for the next six months or so."

"You're diabolical."

"Only sometimes," she admitted. "Besides, these are friends who live across the border and on the other side of the country. This is how I make sure I have people willing to cover me when I commit crimes."

He nodded sagely in response. "Having people willing to be alibis when you break the law is always a helpful thing."

"I don't think that you should be encouraging me in this."

"Well, I should be encouraging you to at least spend more money in the shop."

"You don't think this is enough to justify the amount of time I've spent in here?"

He shook his head. "You're browsing back issues, I don't expect you to spend any money, really. You're not even going for variants."

"Screw variants," she spat. "Useless waste of paper."

"You're not a collector, are you?"

She shook her head. "Dude, I read my comics as a kid until they fell apart. Bags and boards are useless. I'm the kind of person who will buy trades and chop apart the singles for wrapping paper."

"Blasphemy. I don't think we can be friends."

"But I'm so much fun to hang out with," she replied with a grin. "I cook, I feed my friends, and I am a terrible influence in general. I tend to get people sugar high and send them off on random adventures unintentionally. I buy my friends comics and get them signed."

"I work in a comic shop, it's not that big of a deal for me."

"Totally understandable," she said.

"And I cook, I am an adult, after all."

"Yeah, but I cook for a living, so I'm pretty decent at that."

"I've been an adult for a while, I'm pretty good at cooking."

She chuckled. "But I mean, there are other advantages to being my friend."

"Like what?"

She shrugged. "I dunno, I'm not my friend."

"That's extremely self-aware of you."

"I try, dude," she replied with a grin as her phone buzzed in her hand. "'Scuse me a second?" She pressed the screen, typing a response to the message and tucking the phone back into the pocket of her skirt. She picked up two of the issues she'd laid out on the drawer, and put the rest back in numerical order before closing the drawer and turning back to the comic jockey.

"Got what you need?"

"For them," she said with a shrug. "And I guess I got my two favourite covers for myself."

"You… didn't have copies of the books already?"

She sighed and shook her head. "Long story."

"Trades? Or Digital?"

"Sometimes both," she replied sheepishly.

He shrugged. "Definitely not a collector."

"You must already hate me."

"I hate everyone, it comes with the territory."

"I guess I'll try harder," she mumbled.

"Sorry?"

"Never mind."

He arched an eyebrow but let her comment go. "You need anything else?"

"I'm definitely going to get some more current comics for myself. It's been a while since I've actually bought anything."

"Sounds good, let me know if you need any more help?"

"I'm pretty sure I can find Spider-Man comics if I try," she teased.

"There's like a hundred different Spider-Man titles right now," he pointed out. "Besides, you really don't wanna start with anything right this very second, everything is getting re-launched in a few weeks."

"Really?"

"Yeah, at least the one. We dunno what's happening with the other publisher yet. How long has it been since you've bought comics?"

"Shut up. I've never followed anything that closely. I just buy things with pretty art on the cover and then am terribly disappointed with the story and interior art."

"Well, get the things you want signed, then, and hold off on starting anything just yet."

"So you're actively talking me out of spending more money?" she teased. "That's somehow chivalrous of you."

"Chivalry has nothing to do with it. All the runs I like right now are ending in the next two weeks so I haven't got any reason to try and upsell you on things that are ending. Just wait,

I'll make you buy stuff next time you're here. Besides, you're obviously on a mission."

"I read mostly trades," she reminded him.

"Oh right, you're the reason comics go and die before their time."

"Because I read trades?"

"Because you don't buy single issues."

She laughed. "And my one copy of the books I might otherwise consider buying on a regular basis is the reason that books get cancelled."

"Yes. Your buying habits are the reason why all the books that don't deserve it get cancelled, specifically."

"I am truly a terrible person," she agreed, deadpanning to match his tone and sarcasm.

He smiled again and she couldn't help but notice how straight his teeth were, or how the corners of his eyes wrinkled when he smiled. She'd worked her fair share of retail jobs, she knew a fake, polite smile when she saw one, and he wasn't faking his amusement for the sake of hopefully getting her to buy more things.

Oh right, she *was* on a mission, and she'd gotten distracted.

"So I guess I should maybe hold off on getting Spider-Man this week?" she asked.

"Wait 'til after the comic convention," he suggested. "And don't buy the trades there. They'll all be overpriced."

"This isn't my first rodeo," she said. "But yeah, I think I'll hold off on buying anything else today, just grab the other current issues I want signed, and then I'll get out of your hair."

"Sounds good, shout if you need anything."

She watched him walk back to his position manning the register, biting her lower lip and silently chiding herself for watching as closely as he had been. He was cute all right, and clever, and she wondered how much of that was just his retail work persona shining through. She hadn't been kidding when she said she didn't miss working retail. She'd had her fair share of horror stories come from previous jobs, and she'd at one point built the same kind of joking persona to keep customers happy and to keep herself sane. He was friendly though, which was saying something, as the store in general didn't buy in to the entire community kind of mindset. They weren't all gatekeeping elitists, but they weren't the most welcoming kind of comic shop, either. She'd just been going there for so long, in random intervals, that it was habit to go shop there. She was very thankful that she still shopped there and she sent a silent thank you to the universe for giving her the eye candy that was this new guy at her usual comic shop.

The store was dead, there were no customers other than her, and she debated on staying longer, but the buzzing of another message on her phone made her change her mind. It's not like she had much of anything to do, but she was starting to feel like his politeness was wearing thin and she was overstaying her welcome. Instead, she picked up the issues of the comics she was hoping to get signed from the shelf, and made her way to the till.

"Really?" he asked as he saw the titles she'd chosen.

"What?"

"It's just that you have totally random back issues…"

"I like the covers, they're not for reading."

"Yeah, but these ones… Are you actually reading them? I mean, there's a lot better titles you could be getting."

"This is what I'm getting signed," she replied, arching her eyebrow. "And maybe I'll think about reading the rest of the series if it doesn't suck in three issues… which, I mean, It shouldn't 'cause of the writer, but you never know. Why? You gonna judge me for that, too?"

"Hero worship is unhealthy."

"Says the guy who makes a living selling superhero funny books."

He opened his mouth once to reply, then thought better of it. He nodded instead and his mouth crooked in a smirk. "Touché. Nicely played."

She dropped a curtsy. "I try."

"Have fun at your convention."

"I will, definitely. And then I'll come back after and tell you all about it."

"You know, I'd actually like that."

"Yeah? Hard to gauge how sarcastic you're being."

"I'm not."

She smiled. "I'm Emma."

"Scott."

"Charmed."

"I need money," he said.

"You're not a cheap date, are you?" Emma teased.

He didn't respond to that, just shook his head with smirk, and Emma handed over her debit card to pay for the comics she was buying. He bagged her purchase and handed it over. "Thanks. See you 'round."

"Yeah, there's a reboot coming up, I'll be back for that for sure."

"Oh good, I look forward to seeing you."

"I'll make sure to bring you photos of all the half-naked cosplayers."

He snorted and shook his head. "Dude, that's what the Internet is for."

"Gross," Emma replied, rolling her eyes.

"You offered," he reminded her.

"True," she agreed. "But wouldn't you rather some pictures all for yourself?"

"Now who's the gross one?"

"I learned to play with the boys a long time ago. You don't grow up in the 90's reading comics without learning how to sling mud."

"God, we're old."

"We're late-nineties kids, right?" Emma asked. "I mean, you're not like sixteen or something are you?"

"Oh no, I'm *much* older than that."

"Oh, thank God."

"I'm twenty-three."

"Oh, you're way too old for me to even be talking to," she said. "Stranger danger, man."

"Get the hell out of my store," Scott said. "And don't get murdered on the way back from your expo."

"See ya'," Emma agreed with a wave as she walked out of the store, the door opening again with its lonely 'bing-bong.'

She couldn't help but grin to herself the whole way home.

CHAPTER TWO

The convention floor was packed, as usual, and Emma was feeling wildly claustrophobic and confined. Her tight-fitting fake leather jacket for her costume, and the hot wig she was wearing didn't do much to help ease her discomfort. She sighed as she passed yet another group of people dressed up as well-known and iconic characters posing for a photo for some rabid fan and took off the mask that covered most of her face. Her friend beside her handed Emma her glasses and chuckled.

"Hey, at least the people who mattered recognized your costume."

Emma groaned to herself and put her glasses back on before stopping in her tracks to tie her mask onto her head like a fascinator. "I guess so, but you'd think that I'd at least get stopped for one photo, rather than getting asked who the hell I'm supposed to be at every turn."

"Considering that you're a gender-swapped version of the character?"

"Shut up, Sammy."

Sammy laughed and tucked her hair behind her ears. "It's not that big of a deal is it?

You were out to impress one person and they were wildly impressed. Then you got all your comics signed and a photo op and an invitation to hang out later, so why are you so distracted?"

"I'm not distracted," Emma complained. "I'm uncomfortable."

"Wanna go back to the car and change?"

"No."

Sammy laughed and shifted her shopping bags in her arms. "Look, it's really obvious that you're distracted. You didn't even freak out when you met your comics hero."

"I never freak out," Emma replied, scowling. "I get a little tongue tied sometimes, but I don't freak out."

"You never shut up, is what you mean," Sammy teased. "You ramble and it's adorable. You didn't do it this time. What's up?"

"I'm distracted by all the people, and by how uncomfortable being in costume is. I forgot how much it sucks to wear a costume that doesn't breathe."

"Uh-huh, and I'm secretly a Russian super soldier. Come on, how long have we known each other? I've seen you go through a lot of shit; you can't pull the 'I'm just uncomfortable in this skin-tight pair of pants' routine on me. This isn't even the most uncomfortable costume you've ever worn. Remember the plate mail?"

Emma shuddered at the memory of the ill-fitted plate mail armour she'd worn once for a costume. "Okay, fine, you win there. I can't say that I'm so uncomfortable I'm distracted, but to be fair, there's a lot going on in this convention hall and I still need to find gifts for everyone at home…"

"But there's something else on your mind, what is it?"

Emma sighed and scratched her head, groaning under her breath in relief - wigs were never very comfortable and she was getting increasingly irritated by the fact that she was still wearing hers. "Okay, let's go get something to eat and find a place to sit and I'll tell you."

"Deal," Sammy agreed, grabbing Emma's wrist and confidently leading the way through the packed convention hall. Emma followed along helplessly, ignoring the other cosplayers and all the vendors. She wasn't lying about being uncomfortable, she'd not had time to break in the shoes she'd bought, she hadn't brought a spare pair, she'd forgotten to bring any snacks or a water bottle, the jacket she was wearing was tighter than anything else in her normal wardrobe, and the fake leather didn't breathe. They'd been at the convention for six and a half hours, and they'd not stopped for anything since breakfast. She was feeling an increased level of claustrophobia and she felt like the walls were going to crush her.

20

Plus she felt like she was sweating off all her makeup and feeling like she didn't look as good as she had thought she did when she saw herself in the mirror that morning, but she wasn't going to admit to all of that. Fear was the mind-killer, after all, and nobody in the convention knew her anyway, it didn't matter. She'd accomplished what she'd come for and that was all that mattered.

It didn't take long for Sammy to find the food court. Still dragging Emma along by the wrist, she beelined for the nearest empty table and dropped her shopping bags underneath it.

"Okay, sit your ass down," Sammy instructed. "I'm gonna get food and then you will tell me what the hell is going on with you."

Emma groaned and did as she was told, tucking her bags underneath the table and taking a seat. She hadn't realized how badly she needed to sit and let out a little groan of relief as she got off her feet. She pulled her wallet out of her pocket and handed Sammy twenty dollars. "My treat," she insisted.

"Not gonna argue myself out of a free lunch," Sammy agreed with a wink. "I'll be back."

Emma grunted her reply and leaned back in her seat, closing her eyes as Sammy disappeared into the crowd. Emma's stomach rumbled, loud enough for her to be embarrassed, and she tried to ignore the smells of cooking fast food assaulting her while she willed Sammy to hurry up.

It felt like forever, but Sammy returned carrying a pizza box and a tray with two paper cups that rivalled the largest size from a movie theatre. Emma's mouth set to watering immediately as Sammy set the tray down first and Emma only noticed the spicy curly fries in between the giant cups once the tray hit the table.

"You're amazing," Emma muttered, helping herself to the fries and dipping them in the ketchup cup tucked into the tray.

"I know," Sammy replied, setting the pizza box down and opening it. "Pepperoni extra cheese. Still your favorite?"

"Marry me," Emma teased.

"You say that once a year."

"We only see each other maybe once a year," Emma pointed out.

"So isn't marriage a bit sudden?"

"I mean, we've been friends for like ever, I don't think taking this relationship to the next level is entirely unheard of."

"Yeah, but how are we going to explain to our parents that we've suddenly become attracted to one another after all these years and also that we're just in it for the tax breaks?"

"There are tax breaks involved in getting fake married? Why didn't we do that sooner?"

"Something something, I like boys way too much, no offence."

"Oh honey, don't even apologize, I cannot argue that certain men would look far better in the outfit I'm wearing than I do, and I've never had cleavage this nice before."

Sammy laughed and dished out a slice of pizza for Emma, handing it to her before tucking in to her own. The girls ate in companionable silence and Sammy waited until they'd each gotten a single slice of pizza into their stomachs before asking the pressing questions.

"Okay, so now that you're not going into hypoglycemic shock, tell me what the hell is going on with you."

Emma shook her head and sipped the Coke her friend had brought her. "It's stupid," she mumbled.

"It's never stupid with you. Maybe a little insane, but rarely stupid."

"Thanks for the confidence," Emma muttered, rolling her eyes.

"You're wearing a costume that was originally drawn on a buff as hell man who dresses up like a biker with a cat fetish, and you're whining about confidence boosters?"

Emma laughed. "Okay you've got me there, I'm a little insane."

"As long as we agree. So, you gonna tell me what is up with you?"

"Nothing."

"No seriously," Sammy said, helping herself to the fries. "You're not normal today. What's going on? Did someone die?"

"No one died," Emma laughed. "No, it's kinda dumb as hell and I hate it and it's pointless and stupid and I've been distracted 'cause… I dunno."

"Oh."

"Oh what?"

"It's a boy, isn't it?" Sammy deadpanned.

"What? No! Kind of. How did you even know?"

"Please," Sammy replied with a smirk. "You're either daydreaming about a boy or worrying about something that you have absolutely no control over and are being neurotic about. And since you're smiling, and have a faraway look on your face, I'm guessing it's a boy."

"I'm not neurotic!" Emma argued.

"You're a half step away from panic over a boy, to the point where you barely freaked out over meeting your hero."

Emma frowned and took a long pull of her soda.

"Oh. My. God."

"What?"

"There really *is* a boy! Holy crap, Emma. How long has it been since the last one?"

"Last one what?"

"Boy!" Sammy all but squealed. "You've been single for too long."

"I've been single for like three years."

"And that is far too long for someone like you."

"Someone like me?"

"Yeah, you're a serial dater."

"I'm irrevocably single," Emma corrected.

"And you always have long-term relationships that end badly for you," Sammy teased. "But there's a boy. Finally. Is he hot? Is he nice? Where'd you go? Why isn't he here with you?"

"There's no boy," Emma complained. "I mean, well, there is, but I've only just met him and he doesn't even know that I exist outside of the one time we've had a conversation."

"One conversation is a good start," Sammy replied, helping herself to another slice of pizza and putting another on Emma's paper plate. "So where'd you meet him?"

"Comic shop," Emma sighed, running her hand over her face as she felt her cheeks flush with embarrassed heat. "When I went to get the stuff I wanted signed."

"Oh so he's a big nerd, too? Even better!"

"Shut up."

"No way, you've been distracted and now you're all but drooling. Is he hot?"

Emma shrugged.

"Does he have a name?"

"Yes, he has a name. I promise you he actually exists."

Sammy laughed. "Okay, so what's his name?"

"Why do you care?"

"I care because my best friend, who I've known for*ever* is drooling over a boy she just met and won't even tell me what his name is! I need to make sure this guy is on the level, I can't let you go running around willy-nilly with some jerk!"

"You don't even live in the same city as me anymore," Emma pointed out. "I took the bus to get up here. It's not like you're ever gonna meet the guy."

"I still need to stalk him a little and live vicariously through you!" Sammy teased. "Now 'fess up! I want to know all the details."

"There are no details to give," Emma whined. "He's tall, dark hair, narrow nose, you know my type."

"Very well."

"And he's funny," Emma said with a dreamy sigh. "And I've only talked to him the once because he happened to be at the same comic shop I've been going to since forever and he's new there apparently, since I've never seen him before, and… we kinda just joked around while I looked for the back issues I had signed. That's pretty much it."

"That's less exciting than I had hoped."

"I told you that there wasn't really anything to tell."

"But you're distracted as hell."

"He's really cute."

The two friends stared at each other across the table for a long moment before breaking out into a fit of giggles.

"You're hopeless," Sammy said. "You're what, twenty-three now?"

"Shut up."

Sammy shook her head. "Relax. You're fine. At least you didn't say something stupid or drool on yourself when you saw him."

"I'm sure I said a bunch of stupid stuff," Emma sighed. "And I guess I'm going back to the shop to buy comics now."

"And that's the only reason you're going to buy comics?"

"Well, there's a reboot coming up, with new titles and series and… yeah. It's his fault."

Sammy started to laugh again. "You're such a fake geek girl."

"I am a sucker for cute boys. There's a reason why I like Nightwing."

"It's the spandex and that booty, right?"

"Pretty much."

Sammy shook her head. "Are you taking him a gift then?"

"God no."

"So just for the family left?"

"Just the impossible to shop for sister, yeah."

"What about the roommate?"

"He can suck it."

Sammy laughed. "But first, I think you need to finish eating.

Emma looked at her plate where the second slice of pizza lay half-eaten and was rapidly congealing. "Yeah, you're right. Then the last of the shopping, and then you've gotta get me to the bus stop so I can get home."

Sammy saluted and picked up her slice of pizza. "To cute boys," she toasted.

Emma shook her head. "To cute boys," she echoed toasting in return with her cup.

CHAPTER THREE

It was a whole other week after the convention before Emma was able to get back to the comic shop. Her stomach was in knots as she walked back into the store. Between the excitement of the convention, getting everything she'd had signed ailed off to the appropriate friends across the country, and working extra hours to make up for the time she'd taken off to actually get to the convention in the first place, she hadn't had a chance to go and check out the new comics that had been coming out. She was excited to be back, and she couldn't help but hold her breath in anticipation as she rounded the corner and peeked behind the counter.

Scott was standing there, typing something into the computer system and he looked up as he noticed that Emma had entered the store. His face split into a bright smile. "Hey, Emma!"

Holy shit, he remembered my name.

Emma smiled back and set her bag on the floor next to the counter. "Hey."

"You made it back from your show in one piece, that's good."

"Yeah," Emma said slowly as she walked around the counter into the proper store, peering around at the empty facility. "Slow day?"

Scott shrugged. "It's not Wednesday."

"No, it's a Friday afternoon."

"Yeah, and it probably won't pick up for another couple of hours."

"So, then it's probably better that I'm here now so I can harass you for suggestions about what to pick up?"

Scott grinned. "Is that *all* you wanna harass me about?"

Emma pressed her lips together as she felt her face turn red. "The immediate answer I have to that is something wholly inappropriate to say in the store while you're working."

"Please, as if that's ever stopped me from being inappropriate."

"Don't wanna get you in trouble."

Scott fixed her with an incredulous stare and ran a hand through his hair. "We're in a comic shop, short of killing a customer or otherwise harassing someone and getting a complaint, I don't think there's really anything we can say in a mutually joking conversation that will get me in trouble." He peered around the store and made a sweeping motion with his hand. "Besides, does it look like there's anyone here who would complain about anything you could possibly say?"

Emma nodded up at the cameras. "Your boss is probably watching right now."

Scott laughed aloud. "Oh, yeah, and I'm gonna get in so much trouble. How long have you been coming here?"

"Coming here to bug you, specifically? Or to pick up comics in general?"

"Both is good, I suppose," Scott said, "but one is more relevant to the conversation than the other."

"Fair enough," Emma teased back. "A while."

"So then you've probably heard the weird as hell conversations that have gone on in this store, between staff and customers. As long as I'm not being too fully distracted from my job…"

"So I should probably not stand here and distract you too much?" Emma interrupted.

Scott laughed. "Oh, you're a pleasant distraction, don't worry. And I have *so much* work to do today."

"Was that sarcasm?" Emma asked.

"Just a little bit."

"Well I mean, if you've got work to do, then I can browse until I figure out what I want to read."

"I thought we just established that I haven't got much of anything to do at the moment?"

"I'm never really sure with you."

"So really though, comics?" Scott asked.

"Eventually," Emma agreed. "I have pictures of half-naked cosplayers if you're interested."

"Really?" he asked, grinning. "I didn't think you would make good on that one."

"Well…" Emma hesitated, pulling her phone out of her pocket. "I only took a couple of photos of the half naked ones, there were way cooler costumes that I thought you'd appreciate more."

"Show me?"

Emma obliged without hesitation. She pulled up the photo album and scrolled through the photos making a face to herself as she did.

"What's that look for?"

"There's some shit on here I'd rather you not see."

"What? Like nudes?"

Emma snorted and shook her head. "Ha, you wish. No, just random things I've saved off the internet that could probably be used as evidence against me if the need ever arose."

"So like half naked photos of celebrities you're embarrassed to admit to."

"Something like that," Emma agreed absently as she looked through her photos. "But you can look at these ones."

Scott leaned forward until he was resting on his elbows on the counter Emma turned so that he could look over her shoulder at the photos on the phone. "What are those guys?" he asked, touching the screen as he looked at one photo.

Emma shrugged. "I dunno, I thought the costumes were cool. Probably some anime thing."

"Oh, like Attack on Naruto?"

Emma laughed. "What?"

"Yeah, that's the one with the ninja robots that attack half naked giants and use the powers of the dragon orbs to resurrect aliens who come from another planet to enslave mankind, right?"

"I'm honestly not sure how much of that was sarcasm?" Emma asked slowly, making a grimace of confusion as she tried to piece together what he'd actually just said.

Scott laughed. "That's like all I know about anime."

"That's like five things kind of thrown together," Emma replied. "Like, I think I can pick them apart, but you forgot to include some magical girl sailor senshi references in there."

"Shit."

"You fake geek girl," Emma teased.

"Hey," Scott warned with a smirk. "I work in a comic shop, not an anime shop. We don't deal with that crap."

"What have you got against anime?"

"Nothing. I just don't like it."

"Have you tried…"

33

"No. And every time my anime friends try to convince me to watch something, I watch like two episodes and then drink heavily and threaten to kill someone. Suffice it to say I haven't found anything that I like. No, wait," he backtracked, frowning. "There's like one that I've seen all the way through and I enjoyed it but you don't get to know what it is."

"Why not?"

"Because it will ruin my street cred."

"Wow, don't ever say that again," Emma suggested with a forced shudder. "That was… wrong on so many levels."

"Should I go back to talking about Attack on Naruto then?"

"Wouldn't you rather look at this costume of Spider-Man reimagined as Captain America?"

"Hell yes I would," Scott agreed.

"I'd prefer that reboot, actually."

"You would," Scott teased. "You probably have terrible taste in comics."

"Because I'm a girl?"

"Because everyone has terrible taste in comics and it makes all the ones that I like get cancelled long before their time and I'm left with short runs that aren't complete in a way that satisfies me."

"So entitled, aren't you?"

"Work in a comic shop," Scott suggested. "You'll get entitled as hell, too."

Emma arched her eyebrow and smirked. "All retail makes you entitled. You get tired of dealing with people and their demands and it gets irritating and you just wanna snap…"

'Whoa, calm down Miss Vigilante. You're not quite old enough or evil enough to threaten to kill customers."

"Good luck doing retail at Christmas," she deadpanned back. "If you make it without wanting to murder someone for the littlest thing, then you can give me shit for being jaded about retail in general."

"Aw, shit, that's coming up, isn't it?"

Emma chuckled. "Yep. And, dude I got out of retail, I've served my time, never again, if I can avoid it."

"So where do you work, then?" Scott asked.

"Somewhere you can never come find me," Emma said.

"You underestimate my ability to travel between dimensions."

"I work in a kitchen, in a long term care facility. You literally can't come find me unless you have family there and decide that you wanna stalk me or something."

"That sounds wildly underwhelming."

"The work I do?" Emma asked. "Or stalking me at work?"

"Can I say both without you leaping over this counter and strangling me?"

"Hey, I'm not dealing with people buying crap that they can't afford for people who won't appreciate it and freaking out over bills in January," Emma pointed out as she put her phone away. "All I have to do is make sure that the food I'm cooking is at the right temperature and occasionally wash mountains of dishes. It could be worse. I could be doing retail in a comic shop during Christmas."

"You're not gonna let me forget that Christmas is in like six weeks, are you?"

"Not anymore, no."

"You're terrible."

"I'm a good influence on people in the worst kind of way," Emma corrected with a grin.

Scott scowled. "Go get your filthy comics and get the hell out of my store."

Emma laughed. "I actually have no idea what I'm here for," she admitted. "I showed up to show you cosplay photos. Spending money was secondary to coming to harass you. So, with that in mind, you wanna give me some suggestions?"

"Not really," Scott teased.

"Fine," Emma teased right back. "I'm just gonna go touch absolutely everything on the shelves and pick stuff and then put it back in the wrong place."

"Don't you *dare*."

"Don't tempt me, then," Emma said with a devious grin as she wandered away from the counter to meander through the rows of shelves, not giving Scott the chance to argue any more unless he wanted to shout across the store.

Emma heard the phone ring and ignored the conversation Scott was having as she browsed the shelves. She found the rest of the run of her favourite current series and picked up the ones she hadn't collected before getting them signed by the writer. It was odd to her to be picking them up because they were from DC and she usually only read the other guys.

Unsatisfied by the fact that she was only holding three issues of a single title, and wanting to catch up on the rest of the things she'd missed when her interest in comics had waned over the last months, Emma decided she'd give something new a try. She wandered to the new releases wall at the back of the store and browsed, flipping pages to get a feel for the art. She didn't pick any of the new releases up, there was nothing in a series that was numbered below ten and she wasn't in the mood to start something that was likely getting cancelled in the next two weeks when the re-launches happened. It was also a huge deterrent to be staring at issue thirty-five of a run for a character she normally loved, but didn't have the energy, or money, to commit to that many back issues and that much time catching up on the story. She frowned to herself as she couldn't find any decent jumping-on points and she abandoned the new releases to look for something that had familiar characters and less back issues to catch up on.

"You had better not be touching things!" Scott called as Emma moved out of his line of sight.

"I am so touching everything," Emma called back. "And my fingers are totally sticky."

There was a moment's pause and Emma swore she heard Scott trying not to laugh. "…Sticky with what?"

"You don't want to know."

"I might need to know now."

"If I don't answer with 'ice cream' then I guess you can assume that the answer is something else wholly inappropriate to say aloud in the store," Emma said as she made her way to the Marvel section of the store and slipped between the long rows of lovingly alphabetized shelves. "Oh, I think I'm gonna *lick* this one."

That caught Scott's attention and Emma heard him stomping from behind the counter, muttering something under his breath as he walked up beside her.

"Which one are you planning to lick?" he demanded.

"Maybe just this one," Emma said, picking a random comic from the shelf.

"I didn't know you were that into sub-par mutants."

"Hey, you take that back," Emma warned. "They are not sub-par."

"You're seriously not even looking at the comic you're holding," Scott pointed out. "If you did, you'd know that those guys are mostly B-list mutants."

Emma frowned and looked at what random comic she had actually picked up from the shelf. "Oh, Yeah, I don't think I want to lick this one, I might get space cooties or something."

"Space cooties?"

"Or cancer, I dunno, the continuity makes so little sense."

"You're an X-Men fan, aren't you?" Scott asked.

"None of your damn business," Emma shot back.

"If you want suggestions, it kind of is," Scott reminded her with his crooked little grin of amusement.

Emma suppressed a shudder at his adorable smirk. *Dammit, girl, what the hell? You haven't been interested in anyone is four bloody years. Why now? Why him? He's not even that cute.*

Emma silently chided herself, trying desperately not to blush.

Actually, yes, he is *that cute, don't lie to yourself.*

Emma fidgeted in place, frowning and putting the comic back on the shelf while she tried to will away the swarm of butterflies that had taken up residence in her stomach. There was just something about Scott, the way he joked with her, that made Emma super self-conscious. He was cute, sure, and she was highly aware of the fact that she was crushing on him because of looks, but the longer she talked to him, the more she wanted to talk with him. And then she realized how little sense that made.

"You okay?" Scott asked. "You got really quiet."

"Yeah, I'm okay," Emma said, probably a little too quickly, and forcefully, to cover the lie. "Sorry, I just…"

"You're embarrassed, it's cool. Not everyone can admit to what they like. And I mean, you like the X-Men, don't you?"

"Shut *up* about that," Emma whined with a grin. "Actually, yeah, I did, growing up. I guess I still do. Mostly read them and the Fantastic Four when I was younger."

"What? No Batman?"

"No, I don't really like to read those ones."

"Ugh," Scott said with an overly dramatic flip of his hair. "*Brand loyalty.*"

Emma snorted a laugh. "Oh God, actually, yeah, I'm not even gonna try to deny that one. I liked the cartoons and the movies and stuff, but I never really got into Batman in the comics. But I saw Beyond over there, is it any good?"

"It's… not bad."

"But there's something wrong with it," Emma surmised. "I mean I loved the show, it was probably my favorite of the cartoons when I was a kid. Is it super graphic violence or something? 'Cause I mean, I don't dig Joker because he's creepy as hell and super violent. But the concept of the new Beyond run…"

"No, it's a pretty good run, but if you're a fan of the show, you'll be disappointed by it. It's not the same Batman."

"What? It's not Terry?"

"How do you even remember his name?" Scott asked, incredulous and hiding the fact that he was impressed. "I guess, yeah, no it's not Terry."

"You didn't know that was his name, did you?" Emma teased.

"No."

"Fake geek girl."

Scott laughed. "Shit, you figured me out. Don't tell my boss."

"Your secret is safe with me," Emma promised with a shake of her head. "Okay, so I guess I won't read that one, if I'll be *that* disappointed. Maybe I'll wait for the trades."

Scott made a face of disapproval.

"Don't give me shit over that," Emma warned.

"Oh, I'm giving you so much shit over that," Scott replied. "Like, you're going to have to live with the shame of being the reason that comics die. It's your fault. You specifically."

"I feel like you've already tried to guilt me into buying single issues once before," Emma pointed out. "Besides, you don't have all the back issues on the shelves anyway, so I can't start reading a series without the first two issues."

"Sure you can. It's pretty easy to make up a story about what's going on, then just read the rest of the series from there on out."

Emma laughed. "You're weird."

Scott shrugged. "I work in a comic shop, there's a certain level of not-normal we have to have to deal with the rabble that comes in here."

"Rabble?" Emma asked, arching her eyebrow. "That's a phrase I don't hear often."

"I am full of words that are not commonly used in the English language," Scott replied. "The longer you hear me talk, the more you realize I have an extensive vocabulary."

"I would definitely like to hear you talk more."

"That's an invitation for me to never shut up," Scott warned.

"Damn, I fell for your trap." She managed to keep the smile off of her face as she deadpanned her answer back at him. The butterflies in her stomach hadn't toned their tickling tempest down and she was surprised with herself that she'd been able to keep up the conversation as long as she had. He was charming and cute and she didn't usually talk to boys, and she sure as hell didn't *flirt*, but he was different. He was easy to talk to. And was he flirting back? She couldn't tell. He might just be putting up with her because she was willing to spend money, but he was so ridiculous, and genuinely seemed to care.

"You're still not picking comics," Scott pointed out, pulling Emma back to reality and forcing her to ignore the rolling sensation in her guts.

"You're still not telling me what to buy."

"Uh…" Scott stammered, looking over the shelves, pursing his lips. "You don't like violence, so basically you wanna read kids books."

"I never said I didn't like *violence*," she corrected. "I like fun escapist stuff."

"Oh."

"You sound disappointed."

"You probably have terrible taste in comics."

"Because you read highbrow literature?"

"Hell yes I do." His voice was defensive but somehow not serious. "There are comics that absolutely *transcend* the medium and become not just funny books, but actual works of art that will go on throughout time and space and be remembered forever and great works that changed the course of humanity as we know it."

"Okay, so like From Hell. Got it. Yeah, no, I did my time there, I'd like to read brightly colored brain candy, thanks."

"Psh, no, not like that at all." He smirked and flipped his hair dramatically again. "God, you really are such a casual fan."

"I'm going to hurt you in a minute if you keep that up," Emma warned.

Scott smiled. "Oh good, you aren't as shy as I thought."

"What's that supposed to mean?" Emma croaked, feeling the color simultaneously drain from her face as a blush crept into her cheeks.

Scott shrugged. "You're threatening me already and this is only the second time we've talked. Most people get at least to three before they start threatening to kill me."

"How long until they start sexually harassing you?" Emma managed.

"I don't really keep count of that," Scott replied. "Mostly 'cause I know this," he motioned to his face with a single finger, "is the money maker."

"You're an ass."

"I know it," he replied with a grin. "What about Daredevil?"

"Ooh, yeah, I could dig that," Emma agreed.

Scott crouched to where the Daredevil comics were kept. "Okay, so we literally have all ten of the trades of the last run."

"T-ten?" Emma choked. "That's a lot."

"Not really," Scott replied. "But it's numbered stupid, see? They split it so there's two number ones, but it's these ones first, then these." He pointed out the difference in the covers and Emma nodded.

"Okay, but I'm definitely not buying those today."

"Why not?"

"Well," she replied matter-of-factly. "There's ten of them, and they're like what, twenty bucks a piece?"

"Yeah, something like that?"

"So that's two hundred dollars before tax."

Scott's face fell. "Oh, yeah, that's a lot."

"And I kinda would like to eat this week."

"Psh," Scott hissed as he stood. "Food? Who needs that?"

"You're a stick, you're not allowed to joke about food."

Scott looked himself over and shrugged. "Look, we can't all be blessed with long legs and a metabolism that burns like coal."

Emma tilted her head and gave him a look that would have melted his face like acid. "You wanna rephrase that, sentence, there, buddy?"

"I bike everywhere," Scott backtracked. "So...You'd be surprised about how much I don't actually eat."

Emma made a huffing noise but nodded her acceptance of his explanation. "Okay, so I'd like to eat this week, and also pay bills."

"You don't *need* cable."

"I don't have cable TV," Emma replied.

"That's weird."

"Do you have cable?"

"Okay, no, but that's beside the point."

"The point being you want me to spend two hundred bucks on a bunch of comics that I don't necessarily like?"

"You'll like this run of Daredevil, I promise."

"Okay, when I have enough extra cash to come in and buy all of them, I will start reading that run of Daredevil."

Scott wrinkled his face and stood up from where he'd crouched down. "You know I'm going to insist that you buy them every time you come in here now."

"I'm sure you will," Emma replied eyeing the shelves for something that would be interesting to read. "But that metabolism comment didn't win you any points."

"Sorry."

"Not yet you're not," Emma teased, reaching for a comic. "Haven't seen this guy in a comic for a long time, damn."

"And you're not a fan of Captain America?" Scott lamented.

"I like his movies," Emma agreed. "But I'll buy these comics."

"You're *such* a fangirl."

"And you say that like it's a bad thing. Should I buy the Loki bobblehead, while I'm at it?" she asked, nodding up toward the display on top of the comic shelves.

"Ooh, no. That's a waste of money. Did you see the statue at the back of the store?"

"Is it affordable?"

"It's like three hundred bucks."

"So like, more than buying that whole run of Daredevil, which I already refused."

"Yeah," Scott replied with a solemn nod. "But you're a fangirl, you'd drop that money in an instant."

"Yeah, and you're a fake geek girl, it evens out doesn't it?"

Scott laughed. "So you're just going to pick these ones up?"

"Unless you've got some better suggestions?"

"I do," Scott said. "But they're not out 'til the reboot."

Emma snapped her fingers. "Damn, you're oh for two."

"Technically oh for three if you count the three hundred dollar Loki statue I can't convince you to buy."

"Are we keeping score already?" Emma teased. "Because I'm a woman, we never let go of that sort of stuff."

"I'll keep that in mind," Scott agreed. "And I'll stop digging this hole I'm in any deeper by letting you have a free shot."

Emma laughed. "Well, if it makes you feel any better, I've basically not been following anything because I've been stoked about that gothic vampire haunted house movie."

"Oh yeah? Me too. I am actually excited to go see a not-superhero movie for once."

"You wanna go with me?" Emma asked without missing a beat. She felt her heart stop in horror as she realized what she'd just done. Cursing herself, she clenched her teeth and hoped that she hadn't just sounded like a total idiot.

"Yeah," Scott replied, nodding slowly. "I would."

Emma smiled and willed her hear to stop hammering in her chest. "Cool, uh, I guess I'll give you my number then?"

"Sure," Scott replied.

"But uh, do you wanna go grab a coffee with me after work, first?"

"Yeah, let's do that."

"I'll sit in the window so you can find me easy enough."

"I'm going to come over and like, hump the glass and scream at you to buy Daredevil."

"I'm looking forward to you thoroughly embarrassing yourself," Emma said. "I'll just take this pile of comics to go first."

"You sure you don't want Daredevil?"

"I am absolutely certain that I will not be buying Daredevil until you make sweet love to the cafe glass."

Scott nodded. "I'll just ring you up, then."

CHAPTER FOUR

The coffee shop was on the corner, across from the grocery store and only a block away from the comic shop. Emma was giddy as she walked the short distance. She didn't think that Scott was going to say okay. She wasn't even sure what possessed her to ask him for coffee. She's already embarrassed herself enough by asking him if he wanted to go see a movie, and she actually hadn't meant to invite him to that, either. He was just so easy to talk to.

She was practically bouncing when she walked up to the counter to order. The barista smiled as she stared blankly at the menu board above his head.

"Hey, how's it going? Haven't seen you for a couple of weeks!"

Emma looked away from the menu and at the barista. He was young, blonde, and wore thick-framed black glasses. Emma knew that he was one of the newer staff, but he was already her favorite barista. He made the best lattes and she'd always stop in if she saw him through the window. He hadn't quite lost the dedication and care new baristas always put into their coffee making before the need for speedily pumping out drinks made them sloppy. Emma still didn't know his name, though, and the coffee chain didn't make their baristas wear nametags. They hadn't gotten quite that friendly yet.

"Ah, yeah… I haven't been around this area much these past couple of weeks," Emma replied. "I've been busy."

"Read any good books?" he asked.

"Kinda haven't had time," Emma replied with a shrug.

"That's a pity. I read the one you suggested last time, and I loved it."

Emma blinked back her surprise. She'd forgotten that she'd talked books with the barista the last time she'd come in for coffee. "Oh, that's awesome," she managed. "Have you seen the movie yet?"

"Not yet. Is it any good?"

Emma shrugged. "It's as good as a book-to-movie adaptation can be."

The barista laughed. "Fair enough. What can I get for you?"

"I dunno," Emma said. "How much caffeine do I need?"

"How much have you had today?"

"Somewhere between not enough but still under too much."

"Medium vanilla latte it is, then."

Emma laughed. "You remembered my usual?"

"And it's tea if you've had too much caffeine," he replied with a nod. "Usually English Breakfast, but you mix it up with Earl

Grey every now and then. I remember most of our regular customers' orders."

"That's impressive," Emma said, getting out the cash to pay for her coffee. She dropped two extra dollars into the tip jar and moved out of the way as the blonde barista set to making her coffee. It didn't take long for her latte to be ready and she thanked her barista again before shuffling off to her favourite corner seat by the window.

Once she was settled with her coat and bag tucked beside her on the bench, Emma pulled her stack of comics out of her bag. She had a lot of reading to catch up on, and an hour to kill before Scott was off work. She sipped her latte and flipped open the first issue.

The buzzing of her cell phone pulled Emma out of the haze of reading and she blinked stupidly, staring at the phone as she pulled it out of her pocket. The time struck her first and her heart skipped a beat.

6:05

He'd be done closing the till soon. She didn't have long to wait. The text was almost forgotten in her excitement, but a second message came through and reminded her. She opened her phone with a swipe of her finger. The messages were from her roommate.

Hey. Bored. Where you at?

Emma smiled.

No, srsly. Bored. Want me to buy you dinner?

That was an unexpected proposal. Emma and her roommate, Mark, were best friends. They always hung out together and would buy each other dinner all the time. Of course he had to be offering dinner on the one night she'd scored a coffee date with Scott. She hesitated before texting back.

Meeting new friend for coffee by comic shop. Dinner could be good.

It only took a few seconds to get the reply.

Ok. Cool. Be there in 20.

Emma smiled to herself and put the phone back in her coat pocket. She didn't notice the body standing next to her table. She started, stifling a yelp as she looked up.

"God," she grumbled.

"Not quite, but I'm not going to turn down the worship. How much caffeine have you had?" Scott asked with a crooked smirk as he slipped onto the chair opposite Emma.

"What happened to you humping the glass and screaming at me to buy more comics?"

Scott laughed sheepishly. "Ah yeah, I talk big but I lack conviction so a lot of that crap doesn't get followed through."

"That's a damn shame. I'd have liked to watch you make a fool of yourself in an attempt to embarrass me, or guilt me into buying comics. I'm actually surprised that you came out."

"Why?" Scott replied.

"Well, aside from the fact that you just told me you lack conviction to follow things through?" Emma asked. "Because I'm a weird girl who you barely know who randomly asked you out for coffee after spending far too much time harassing you in the store. I mean, if it were reversed, I'd probably have told you to fuck off."

Scott laughed again. "Well, aren't you lucky that you happen to be a weird girl and I'm not really afraid of much."

"I could be a serial killer and you wouldn't know it."

"Gonna bury me in your backyard and grow mushrooms for your fine dining in the kitchen?"

"Ew, no. Mushrooms are gross."

"So then you're just going to murder and eat me. I see how it is. Can't blame you. I'd eat me. I've got lovely thighs from biking everywhere."

Emma's face twisted in disgust and she sipped on the dregs of her tepid latte. "Can't say I'm much of a fan of long pork," she replied.

Scott arched an eyebrow. "No? That's a pity, guess I won't invite you over for dinner."

"I'll definitely not be taking you on the invite home," Emma replied. "I'm quite fond of not getting murdered by cannibals."

"Yeah, it's only fun once."

"For the cannibal murderer or for the victim?"

"Take your pick?"

"You know you'd have better luck if you let your victims stay free-range?" Emma suggested. "Treat them kindly, put them to sleep before killing them. Less stress on the body and the meat stays more tender and doesn't get that nasty chemical taste."

"You talk like you've got some experience in this, and that's the scariest part."

"Told you I'm impressed that you actually took me up on my offer to come to coffee," Emma said, flashing her best creepy grin. "You barely know me, after all."

"I know you like X-Men comics, and that you are mildly disappointed with the ones you picked up today, and that if you were planning on killing and eating me, you'd not do it this close to my work or in your local hangout."

Emma shrugged. "Logical, how'd you know I was disappointed in the comics I picked up?"

"I'm just guessing because you didn't start raving about them as soon as I walked in."

"I have interests outside of comics, and I assume you're highly sick of hearing about comics by the time you're off work. It's a courtesy thing."

"I read thirty-five titles."

Emma's jaw dropped. She couldn't help it. That number was staggering. "How… How do you keep that many ongoing stories straight?"

Scott shrugged. "It's a little more than one comic a day every month. It's not that bad."

"It's a little bad," Emma replied, shaking her head. "I can't even keep continuities straight, let alone thirty-five separate, ongoing stories."

"Good thing you're not paid to give people suggestions to spend more money in the shop, then."

"Damn shame you lack the conviction to actually convince me to spend all of my money in your shop."

"Why don't you just rip my heart out and eat in front of all these people?" Scott teased.

"I'm not a cannibal."

"Oh, am I giving away too many secrets on the first date?"

Date? Emma ignored the word and deadpanned her response back to hide the fluttering of butterflies in her stomach.

"Ah, so you make the cannibal jokes to put your victims at ease so that no one suspects you when you're the last person your victims are seen with?"

"I probably shouldn't have mentioned my mushroom garden," Scott replied, tapping his chin and frowning. "That tends to freak people right the hell out."

"Takes a little more than cannibal jokes to make me run out on a date," Emma reassured him.

"So we're still on for vampire-ghost movie night, then?"

"If you don't mind me inviting another friend who I promised we'd also make a date to go see it," she replied.

"The more the merrier," Scott agreed. "Means neither of us will kill the other in a public place."

"Done deal," Emma said with a smirk that wrinkled her nose. She reached into her coat and handed Scott her phone. "Can I have your number? I'll just text you so you'll have mine."

"Sure."

Emma watched as Scott put his contact information into the phone.

"You have a Captain America phone case," Scott pointed out, unamused. "But you won't buy the comics?"

"I have a lot of Captain America stuff," Emma replied. "He's kind of a corporate sellout. There's a lot of merchandise for him, but not so much for his young ward."

"I don't think anyone has referred to Bucky Barnes as Cap's 'young ward' since the sixties."

"I don't think he's ever actually been the 'young ward'," Emma corrected herself. "Might have been partner. Or just the ambiguous 'young friend' but I can't remember."

"Now who's the fake geek girl?" Scott asked.

"You are," Emma replied, taking her phone back and rapidly typing out a text. "But that's mostly because you're still a dude, as far as I can tell."

"Hey," Scott replied, shaking his head. "Just because I'm not a girl doesn't mean I'm a fake geek."

"I don't even understand your logic half the time," Emma replied.

"That's fine, I don't either."

"So, um…" Emma started as her phone buzzed in her hand. "Um… My roommate is coming to pick me up."

"Roommate?" Scott asked, wagging his eyebrows. "Is she hot?"

"She is a he, named Mark," Emma replied.

"Is he your boyfriend?"

"God, no."

"Oh, is he hot?" Scott asked with an even wider grin.

"He's not bad looking. Depends on your type, I guess?"

"My type is breathing," Scott said.

"You have super low standards, then," Emma said.

"Hey, you don't mess around with your livestock," Scott pointed out.

Emma gagged. "Oh God, that's so gross." She paused as her thought process caught up to her disgust and she came to a crushing realization over the entire joke. "Wait, do you have higher standards for people you intend to eat?"

"Well yeah, d'uh. They have to be breathing and relatively healthy. And dumb enough to trust me."

"No more cannibal jokes!" Emma whined. "So gross."

Scott laughed. "Okay, for now."

"For now," Emma agreed. "So am I dumb enough to trust you?"

"You're the one who invited me out," Scott pointed out. "I'm dumb enough to trust *you*, but you've already said you're not a serial killer so I think I'm in the clear. Do you need to leave then, if your roommate is coming to get you?"

"He kinda owes me dinner, so we were gonna go grab burgers or something, do you wanna join us?"

"Is your roommate gonna kill me in a jealous rage?"

"Mm…" Emma wrinkled her nose as she considered that answer.

"Wow, that's really reassuring," Scott said quickly, and very sarcastically. "I really think that introducing me to your male roommate who you swear isn't your boyfriend is a smart idea. I can't wait to meet this guy who lives with the not serial killer I've agreed to have coffee with - which I'm not currently drinking, by the way."

"Do you want a coffee?" Emma asked, interrupting him before he could finish his rant.

"No, I don't actually drink coffee," Scott replied, losing all the steam and build up from his rant. "But yeah, I'd love to join you for dinner if I'm not intruding or gonna get killed."

"Who's killing whom?"

Emma smiled widely as Mark walked up behind Scott. Scott turned around in his seat to face the other man. Mark was as tall as Scott and thicker, less willowy.

"Yeah, not bad," Scott told Emma with a surreptitious wink.

"Oh God…" Emma groaned, cradling her head in her hands as Scott stood to introduce himself.

"I'm Scott, nice you meet you. I'm assuming you're Emma's roommate?"

"Mark. Hey." He looked at Emma. "So this is your new friend, huh?"

"Yeah," Emma replied. "Play nice, I'm the only one allowed to be mean."

"Is that a house rule?" Scott asked.

"I've known her for like ten years," Mark explained. "It's like a life-with-Emma rule, and she's not even that mean."

"So she just likes to pick on me?" Scott asked as Emma pulled on her coat.

"It's because you're shiny and new," Mark agreed. "She's gotta get some of the polish off before she decides if she's gonna keep you or not."

"Wow, that's nice, Mark, thanks for telling all of my secrets," Emma interjected.

"Keep me? Like in a cage?"

"No, more like a glass case," Emma replied. "But that's only if you're trophy material. If you're not, then it's a cage, but like a really nice one."

"One where I can go outside and engage in natural behaviours? Like one of those free range chickens?"

"Exactly like that," Emma agreed. "Mark is building the pen outside this weekend."

"I can't wait to build a nest," Scott said. "Dinner?"

"Lead on," Mark replied.

Emma grabbed Mark's arm, holding him back as Scott headed out of the coffee shop. "Seriously, be nice, you big jerk."

"I am being nice," Mark replied. "He's cute, I see why you like him. Where'd you meet him?"

"Comic shop."

"Fuckin' nerd."

"Me? Or him?" Emma asked.

"Can it be both?"

"It can be, sure. And I wouldn't talk mister watches cartoons online all night."

Mark laughed and threw his arm over Emma's shoulders, leading her to catch up to Scott, who was standing outside on the sidewalk.

"You get lost?" Scott teased.

"Yeah, I had to stop for directions," Mark replied easily. "Burger joint just down the block is good, you ever been?"

"Nope, but that sounds good."

"How can you work like on the corner over there and not have eaten at this burger joint?" Mark asked. "It's the best place on the strip."

"I work in a comic shop," Scott replied, incredulously. "I don't get lunch breaks."

"Ah yes, the days of retail hell," Mark said with a solemn nod. "I remember those days."

"It's not that bad," Scott replied. "I mean, I work in a comic shop, there are far worse places to work."

"I'll drink to that," Mark agreed.

The burger joint was a small restaurant, cramped with only four tables and a bar against the window. Scott took off his coat and draped it over one of the chairs next to the bigger table and Emma and Mark followed suit. They ordered their meals and waited, sipping Coke from the glass bottles the restaurant served.

"Okay, but seriously, you just what, asked him out?" Mark said loudly, making Emma's face turn bright red.

"She threatened me," Scott replied easily. "Not like that's out of the ordinary, but it's effective."

"Oh my God, I don't know if introducing you two was a good idea or not…" Emma groaned. "You're getting along."

"Uh oh," Mark agreed. "We should probably go fight."

"That requires effort," Scott pointed out. "I'd rather not."

"Getting along it is," Mark replied, toasting Scott with his bottle of Coke.

Emma winced as Mark laughed.

"Would you rather us actually go fight?" Mark asked.

"No, this is fine," Emma said. "I prefer it when my friends get along."

"I've been promoted to friend," Scott exclaimed. "Excellent!"

"Aw man, it took me three years to get that promotion."

"You're such a dick," Emma muttered.

"That's why you still hang out with me after that long," Mark teased. "She's into…"

"Don't finish that sentence," Emma warned as Scott burst out laughing.

Mark flashed Emma an innocent smile and stood as their orders were called. He returned to the table in a minute, expertly carrying the baskets that their burgers were served in, and set them on the table in front of Emma and Scott. "Man, I should have been a waitress."

"You can't walk in heels," Emma pointed out.

"I can walk in heels better than you can," Mark shot back.

"Okay, you don't have enough cleavage to make enough tips to make being a *server* worth your time."

"Do you two always fight like a married couple?" Scott asked. "Or is this just for show 'cause I'm here?"

Emma and Mark exchanged thoughtful looks. They nodded simultaneously and agreed.

"No, this is normal," Emma said.

"All the time," Mark agreed. "She's unbearable. Run while you can."

Emma gave Scott a dead-eyed stare. "At least he hasn't confirmed whether I'm a serial killer or not."

Scott nodded slowly. "Yeah, I think I'll take my chances."

Emma grinned and tucked a loose strand of hair behind her ear. "Good choice."

CHAPTER FIVE

"So you've been awfully quiet today," Stacey said as Emma stirred a pot of soup.

Emma looked up from the rapidly thickening concoction and grinned. "Yeah, I'm a little distracted."

"This isn't your normal lost in thought distraction, what's up?"

Emma laughed and shook her head. She loves Stacey to death. She was older than Emma and was a motherly work friend. They talked about everything when they were in the kitchen together and Stacey had gotten to know Emma very well, very quickly.

"Nothing is up, *mom*," Emma teased.

"Oh, I can tell when something is up with you. You forget that I have kids," Stacey said with a grin and a poke to Emma's shoulder. "What is it?"

Emma shook her head. "God, you're worse than my friends outside of work."

"See? You're not as dark and mysterious as you like to pretend you are."

Emma made an exaggerated, exasperated sigh as she took the pot of soup off the stove and transferred it into a steam table insert. "Oh, you know, just the usual stuff. Money, house, boys."

"The boys bit is new," Stacey observed. "What's going on?"

"There's a boy."

Stacey's face split into a wide, knowing grin. "Ooh, my little Emma has a crush!"

"Shh, don't tell the world."

"Why not?"

"He doesn't know yet."

"Oh please, Emma, boys aren't oblivious idiots."

Emma bobbed her head; she didn't entirely believe that sentiment.

Stacey laughed. "Well that's adorable. What's his name?"

"None of your business."

"Ooh, it's a serious crush 'cause you've got the attitude."

Emma laughed. "What does that mean?"

"It means that I've seen my daughter go through the same thing, and that's fine. It's really cute, but you need to drop the defensive attitude, kiddo."

"Sorry," Emma replied with a sigh. "I'm not quite sure what's going on yet. I mean, he's super sweet and we went out for coffee kind of, I mean, he came with me and my roommate for dinner, so it's not like it's anything other than friendly… anything."

Stacey nodded as Emma carried the insert full of soup to the steam table. She followed her younger friend, adding the inserts she had been filling with the lunch items to the steam table behind Emma.

"So you have a crush on your new friend. And I'm assuming he's adorable?"

"I wouldn't say adorable," Emma started, "but yes. Very much."

Stacey laughed again. "You've got it bad."

"I know, and I hate it."

"You don't *really* hate it."

"I definitely wasn't expecting to get ambushed by feelings like this."

Stacey couldn't help but grin. The frivolities of youth amused her to no end. "Well, I'm happy that you've finally got some feelings about you."

"I've got too many," Emma complained.

"That's why you work here," Stacey teased back. "You wanted to get rid of those feelings."

Emma laughed. "God, working here means I go home crying every other night. You know how it is."

"I do know how it is," Stacey agreed solemnly. "So I'm really happy that you've got an outlet."

"Outlet?"

"Hey, you've been smiling this whole time and you forgot where you are for a little while, right? That's an outlet. You've got something to distract you, and it's obviously making you happy."

"Nothing's going on, though," Emma pointed out.

"Yet," Stacey corrected. "You get his number yet?"

"Maybe," Emma replied, pursing her lips and praying that she wasn't blushing as much as she thought she was.

"So that's a yes, good for you."

"It's nothing," Emma argued. "I have a silly crush. He's cute, he's nice, he's hilarious… I met… him in the stupidest way though, and I don't think it's anything."

"You almost told me his name!" Stacey teased. "Come on, you know you want to spill your guts."

Emma glanced up at the clock on the wall. Almost noon. The lunch rush was about to hit, and then they would have to wash a mountain of dishes before their respective shifts were over.

"It's Scott," Emma said finally, sighing in defeat even as she felt her lips curl into a grin. "I met him at the comic shop I go to. He's new, kind of. I haven't been buying comics for like a year, so I haven't seen him before. I…"

"You're so cute when you're flustered," Stacey teased.

Emma grimaced, wrinkling her face and shaking her head. "I'm not flustered."

"You're definitely flustered."

"Are you sure you're actually old enough to be my mom?" Emma teased.

Stacey laughed as she helped fill the steam table with inserts full of food. "I'm sure I'm old enough to be your mother, but the thing is that I'm not, and you're mature enough to be my friend."

"I can't wait to be old enough to pull that line on some poor young girl who thinks I'm fun enough to hang around with."

Stacey laughed, loud enough to get a weird look from the other cooks preparing the afternoon meal. Stacey shot a challenging look back and no one challenged it.

"So anyway," Emma continued, shaking her head. "I don't know anything about anything."

"Well, good luck. When do you get to see him again?"

Emma sighed. "Wednesday-ish."

"Why Wednesday?"

"New comics come out on Wednesdays."

"That's so dumb."

"Books are traditionally released on a Tuesday," Emma pointed out. "Movies on Fridays."

"So Wednesday. Good for you. You gonna ask him out?"

"I kinda… accidentally invited him to the movies while we were talking, so then he came to have coffee and dinner and we traded phone numbers."

"So you have a date."

"No," Emma sighed. "Not really. Nothing's set in stone and it's one of those things that I was already planning to do with some other friends and I kinda accidentally invited him to come with me."

"Safety in numbers," Stacey pointed out. "You'll be fine. Just go say hi, be yourself, have some fun. You need it."

"I need fun?"

"God yes, you do. This place will make you go insane."

Emma chuckled. "Yeah, all right. I'll have fun."

"Good thing, 'cause this lunch rush is going to suck."

CHAPTER SIX

"Oh it's you." His voice was devoid of all emotion, deadpan and bored. It was a statement of absolute disappointment and the look on Scott's face was blank, completely selling the sentiment.

"Wow," Emma replied as she set down her bag. "Rude."

Scott laughed and leaned against the counter as Emma walked around. The counter was raised and made him even taller than he already was. Emma leaned against the edge of the counter and looked up at him, half-smirk touching the one side of her face, challenging Scott to be that much of an asshole. She had missed their little chats, moving from silly banter, to friendly shit-giving, to flirtatious jokes so quickly that any onlookers would get whiplash if they weren't used to it.

"So you're actually back," Scott said. "I almost didn't think you were going to come get books."

"Dude, why not?" Emma asked. "It's a reboot. I can read *everything* now."

"That's a very good point," Scott agreed. "I just wasn't sure you were actually reading anything."

72

"Nope," Emma agreed. "I just like the pretty pictures. How many titles got launched today?"

"Uh…" Scott frowned and counted on his fingers, mouthing titles as he did. "I think like ten."

"Damn, I'm definitely not reading ten new titles."

"What about the ones you were reading before?"

"None of them really grabbed me, unfortunately," Emma said with a sigh. "Not enough naked superheroes to keep me interested."

"…Are you not reading Thor?"

Emma laughed. "Not really, besides, the old runs of Hercules were the best for consistent, half-naked dudes, and there isn't a current Hercules run."

"That's true, but they're not very good."

"Define good," Emma said. "Do you mean morally upright? Politically charged? Something that you can read more than once and not get bored? Does the art factor into whether something is good in your opinion or are you just about the story?"

"Uh…" Scott stammered. "Well, I mean… Can't it be all of the above?"

"Yeah, that's what I thought," Emma said with a sigh. "I read comics because I want something fun and escapist."

"So you definitely don't like Captain America?"

"I like the movies and cartoons generally better than the comics."

"You are such a fake geek girl," Scott teased.

"And proud," Emma replied, deadpan with a shake of her head. "So what should I get this week?"

"Of the new stuff?" Scott asked.

"No, back issues," Emma deadpanned.

"I can't tell if you're being sarcastic or not," Scott admitted. "You do this deadpan thing, and you just lose all emotion in your voice…"

Emma laughed. "Okay, quit being sarcastic."

"You first."

Emma shook her head again. "You're such a jerk."

"You keep coming back," Scott pointed out. "But if you really don't want to see me, I'm not here on Sundays."

Emma stuck her tongue out at him and turned on her heel to go and browse the new releases section at the back of the store.

"Did you just stick your tongue out at me?" he called as she disappeared between the racks. "You know that's childish, right? And vaguely threatening."

Emma chuckled under her breath as she browsed the racks. He hadn't been kidding, the new release racks were overflowing with more new titles than she'd seen in a long time. A lot of the names she didn't recognize, titles, cover artists and writers were all new and unfamiliar to her and she realized she'd been reading the same things since she was a child, never really venturing out of her comfort zone. She felt momentarily lost as she considered buying TV tie-in comics, but thought better of it when she wasn't thrilled by the art style.

"Oh my God," Emma muttered to herself, "I'm turning into an art snob, aren't I?" She sighed and picked up the comics that caught her eye the most. She wasn't thrilled with the fact that she was holding very tightly to an X-Men comic. And it was even less than thrilling to realize that it was the first one she'd picked up. She had five comics in her hand and she was satisfied with that selection. She didn't even browse the older runs because she knew she would end up picking up something she couldn't afford, and that Scott would be able to convince her to buy something if she gave him an inch.

"Only five?" Scott asked as he rang her purchase through the till.

"You think I should get more?" Emma asked.

"Well not from the big-two, no."

"Do you read a lot of indies?"

"God, I read everything."

"Everything everything?" Emma asked. "Or just your definition of 'everything' because you have a lot of spare time and a staff discount and you're paid to know what's what?"

"Can it be both?"

Emma made a non-committal noise as she handed over her bank card.

"So you got the X-Men."

"Shut up," Emma muttered.

"I'm not saying it's bad, necessarily, just that it's X-Men."

"You say that with such disdain."

"It's X-Men, come on."

"So I probably shouldn't admit to who my favourite characters are then, should I?" Emma asked. "Because, if you're giving me that much shit over my love of the X-Men already, I'm not sure that my poor fragile girl heart can handle being judged so harshly over liking shitty comic book characters."

Scott laughed. "Well, when you put it that way, I absolutely need to know."

"Nope, not telling you."

"Why?"

"Because I have a legitimate list of characters who will make me buy damn near anything that they're in."

Scott grinned and handed Emma her bag. "Okay, now I absolutely have to know."

Emma whined wordlessly and shook her head. "I can't tell you everything up front, that ruins the mystery."

"What mystery?"

"The mystery of what I like."

"But if you tell me," Scott replied slowly, a grin creeping across his face, "then I can tell you what comics you need to buy so that you're not bored."

Emma shook her head; trying to ignore the smile he was giving her. It was cute and alluring and made her stomach roil and flip. "No, I can't afford to but a million comics."

"Pfft, we've been over this. Food is unnecessary."

"No, cable is unnecessary. Food is good."

"Okay," Scott agreed. "I'll give you that one."

"I already had that one," Emma reminded him. "You're just being picky because you're competitive and you hate to lose, especially to a girl."

"Am I that transparent?" Scott exclaimed. "Shit."

"You're not," Emma assured him. "But, now you've just confirmed it so that's another point for me, and you should probably tone it down 'cause I'm just as competitive."

"I like a challenge."

Emma had to repress a shudder of delight. The tone of his voice was low and verging on seductive. She knew he was just screwing with her, but it was just enough to send a chill down her spine.

"I like Doom," she said after a long minute. "And that's all you get to know for now."

"You know he's in like three comic series right now?"

Emma covered her ears with her hands. "Not listening."

"No, I'm serious," Scott said. "Remind me next time and I'll make you buy a bunch more comics."

Emma laughed and nodded. "Deal," she agreed. She took a breath and looked up at Scott, expectantly. "So we're still on for the movies, right?" she asked, suddenly very nervous.

"Yeah, I mean, I thought we were?"

"Well, I kinda forgot that I promised to go see this movie with other friends…"

"Am I not invited?" Scott asked.

"You're totally invited, if you're cool with it being a group thing?" Emma replied.

Scott shrugged. "No harm in that."

Emma nodded. "So, we're going next Tuesday."

"What time?"

"The movie starts at 7:10, unless you wanted to aim for a matinee, then I can text everyone…"

"No, that's perfect," Scott agreed, interrupting. "Don't worry, I'll be there at seven."

"Awesome, I'll just confirm with everyone else," Emma said with a nod. "But, um… Do you wanna come for drinks after work? I'm meeting Mark and another friend, you're welcome to come."

"I… have family stuff to do."

"Oh, yeah? Cool, no big, just thought I'd offer."

Scott smiled. "You know what? Screw it, what's the harm in one drink?"

CHAPTER SEVEN

Emma waited outside the shop for Scott to finish closing for the day. She sat on the wooden steps, waiting. It was pleasant out, the weather hadn't gotten too cold yet, and she couldn't complain. The sidewalk was mostly empty and no one who passed her bothered to stop and ask what she was doing. She smiled as she heard the door open behind her and didn't move when Scott walked down the three steps beside her.

She looked up at him, still unmoving from her spot and flashed him a bright smile. "Man, this is creepy of me, isn't it?"

"What?"

"Waiting on the steps like a stalker."

Scott laughed. "I've had worse."

"I'm not trying hard enough, then."

"Are you sure that's a title that you really want to go for?"

Emma shrugged and stood, brushing dirt off her butt and legs and smoothing out her skirt as she did. "I once got a job by quoting Conan the Barbarian, I'm not sure that it's really difficult for me to be The Worst Person Ever."

Scott laughed. "That's impressive."

"I'm the nicest terrible person you'll ever meet," Emma agreed.

"So what's going on?"

"What do you mean?" Emma asked.

"Like, where are we going?"

"Oh," she replied. "Right."

Idiot, chill out. Emma chided herself. *This isn't a date, it's drinks with friends, God.*

"Um, just to one of the pubs on the other side of the street and around the corner."

Scott made a face. "Not the really hipster English pub, I hope?"

"Naw, that place is always *packed*. We never go there. We're going to the big one down the street from the Irish pub that's always got heavy metal playing."

"Ah, yeah, cool. I've never been there."

"Really?" Emma asked as they started walking.

"Yeah, I haven't really worked my way down the street to eat yet. I don't really have time to sit for a long meal during work, so if I don't pack a lunch, it's grocery store deli stuff."

"Nothing wrong with that," Emma agreed. "So you cook, then?"

"I'm a damn good cook," Scott agreed. "Kinda have to be when you live alone. Why?"

"Just wondering," Emma said with a nonchalant shrug. "I mean, we've only had like what? Five conversations in the store? There's a lot to talk about, isn't there?"

"I guess so," Scott agreed. "So you cook?"

"I'm a girl and that's what I do for a living. Of course I cook," Emma replied with a laugh. "What kind of question is that, even?"

"Well, if you cook, why are we going out to get drinks?"

Emma felt her heart skip a beat and her stomach flip. What kind of question was that? She opened her mouth and then closed it again, frowning as she tried to come up with an answer to that, though nothing clever was easily forthcoming and she was forced to resign herself to being quiet for a longer moment than anticipated.

"Is this is fast as you walk?" Scott asked suddenly, as if he was acutely aware of the mild discomfort lingering in the silence.

"Excuse you?"

"I mean, good Lord, you're slow."

"I'm slow?"

"Yeah, look," Scott explained, picking up his pace as he lengthened his stride and walked to the end of the block and back again before Emma had barely moved ten feet. "You are *so slow*."

"Oh, I'm sorry that I'm only five-foot-seven and don't have massively long tree-like limbs," Emma shot back, trying very hard not to laugh. "It's not like I can magically make myself taller or anything."

Scott made an exaggerated sigh and flipped his hair. "God, you're so selfish. Being short and not having magic powers, what's wrong with you?"

Emma laughed at that, she couldn't help it. "Do you want an itemized list?"

"Would it help?"

"It would definitely give you more legitimate reasons to get up and run the hell away from me," Emma agreed.

"So you're actually a serial killer then?"

"Sure," Emma said. "If that's what you wanna believe."

Scott quirked an eyebrow but didn't press the matter. "Well, at least you're honest about being a psycho."

"I'm a girl, I'm probably at least ten percent psycho."

"Only ten?" Scott asked, tapping his chin. "Yeah, okay, we can be friends."

"Ouch," Emma replied, clasping a hand over her chest. "That's painful, you'd not be friends with me if I was more of a psycho?"

"Yeah, something like that. I mean, twelve percent psycho is just out of the question."

"Well, don't worry, I'm not that crazy," she promised. "I'm just a little crazy. Just enough to keep things interesting."

Scott snorted a laugh. "Interesting, huh? I'll keep that in mind."

"It's a warning," Emma replied with a smirk. "You either love it, or you run."

"Sounds like a challenge."

"Definitely not a challenge," Emma promised. "I'm sure you could run very far, very quickly, and I'd never see you again."

"Until you come and get comics."

"I can always start coming in on Sunday."

"You could," Scott agreed. "But then you'd be missing all of this." He made a general sweeping motion over his whole body and flashed a grin. "And somehow I don't think you *really* want to start going to the store on Sunday. It's boring on Sunday."

"Okay, then I won't bother going to the shop on Sunday."

"Good choice," Scott said. "Is this the pub?"

"Yep," Emma agreed, pulling out her phone as they loitered on the sidewalk. "Let me just text my friends and see where they're at."

"Someone's waving at you," Scott said, nodding over Emma's shoulder.

Emma turned around to look and she grinned, shaking her head. "Well never mind, that's them."

Two young men were walking down the street. They were both tall and slim, though shorter of the two was wider in the shoulders. It took Scott a moment before he recognized

Mark. They walked up to Emma and she hugged them both in turn.

"You brought a stray?" the shorter of the two asked.

Emma laughed. "This is Scott, and yes."

"Hey," Mark said. "Nice to see ya. This is Dave."

Dave gave a nod in Scott's direction. "'Sup?"

Scott shrugged. "Not much."

"Cool," Dave replied with a nonchalant shrug. "Booze me," he said with a crooked grin before leading the way into the bar.

It wasn't very busy inside the bar and the group had no trouble getting a booth near the window. Mark and Dave slid into the curved booth first, Scott followed and Emma took the edge of the seat next to Scott.

"This your usual hangout?" Scott asked.

Emma shrugged. "Depends on the day but it's usually pretty quiet in here."

"Except after seven on a Friday or Saturday night," Mark added. "Food's good though, and it's pizza night so that's what we're ordering."

"You got any preference for toppings?" Dave asked.

Scott shook his head. "Just not pineapple."

Dave gave him a thumb's up across the table as the waitress appeared.

"You guys ready to order?"

The boys all ordered beer, Emma ordered a Coke, and Mark and Dave took it upon themselves to order food.

"Not drinking?" Scott asked.

"No. I don't really drink."

"You don't drink?"

Emma shook her head. "Not really. Don't worry about it."

"I'll drink Coke if you'd rather…"

"Why?" Emma asked. "Everyone else is having a beer. I just don't drink. It's not a big deal to me."

"You sure?"

"Positive. This is normal. Go ahead. I honestly don't care."

"So, Scott, who the hell are you?" Dave asked as the waitress returned with their drinks.

"A cyborg from the future."

"Cool," Dave replied with an approving nod. "So what do you do then, as a cyborg from the future? Who are you supposed to murder?"

"Dunno yet," Scott explained. "So I work over at the comic shop."

"Comics, huh?" Dave drawled. "Let me tell you a thing about comics."

Emma groaned under her breath as Dave launched into a tirade she'd heard about a hundred times. Dave was a big comic nerd, and he had Opinions about them. The capital letter was warranted, and was audible whenever he started talking about them. At least Scott was able to keep up and he argued almost every point, working Dave up and keeping him engaged even as their pizzas were brought to the table. Between Emma and Mark, Scott's plate was never without a slice of pizza and Scott didn't complain, he just kept pace with the arguments Dave was making, getting more animated as the conversation got more heated.

As the conversation went on and she stopped caring, Emma leaned back against the booth, giving to attention to Dave's arguments about gender politics about a movie she'd not seen yet and the comic book tie in, and surreptitiously drew her phone from her pocket. She tapped the screen, holding the phone on her lap, under the table, and grinning at the conversation she'd just started. Mark had been playing on his phone the whole time, tuning out Dave's conversation. His face lit up in a grin and he tapped out a response, shooting Emma a look across the table.

"Are you guys texting?"

Emma and Mark both looked over to their companions. It was Dave who had asked. Mark shrugged and Emma grinned.

"Wait, are you two texting *each other*? What the hell is wrong with you?"

"You guys are talking a lot of shit that I have no interest in," Emma replied. "And I haven't seen either of the movies you keep picking apart, so I have nothing to add to this conversation."

"And I have no idea what you nerds are even going on about," Mark added with another shrug before taking a gulp of his beer. "To be fair, I was looking at the internet before Emma started texting me."

"No point in shouting over the music and you two," Emma added.

Scott laughed. "Ah, the misuse of technology at its finest."

"You wouldn't have known if we weren't laughing," Emma pointed out.

"That is a fair assessment," Scott agreed.

"I need a smoke," Dave announced. "Comic Boy, you want to smoke?"

"I don't smoke, haven't for ever."

"You can pull a Sherlock and just watch me smoke and live vicariously through me, then."

Scott laughed. "Yeah, okay."

Dave made a clicking noise with his tongue and a gun with his fingers, and got up, Emma moved out of Scott's way to let him follow. She watched her friends exit the bar, taking up the standard smoker's position outside on the sidewalk. She shook her head, watching through the window as the boys started talking animatedly while Dave smoked.

"Yeah, you can keep him," Mark said, watching Emma watch the boys outside.

"I didn't realize that I needed your approval," Emma replied.

"Eh, he's all right, and he keeps Dave occupied," Mark said with a smirk. "I'm glad you're making new friends, too. Your old ones are kinda boring."

Emma fixed Mark with an incredulous look. "You do realize that you're pretty much my only friend, right?"

"I'm in the top three at least," Mark agreed with a grin. "Movie night is fine, by the way," he added, referencing their text conversation. "I talked to Luna between texting you, and it's all arranged."

"Cool," Emma agreed, tucking her phone back into her pocket as the others came back in.

"One more round?" Dave asked as Emma slid over to let Scott sit on the edge of the booth.

"I'll have another, sure," Mark said easily, "but that's it, I'm driving."

"It's been like a hundred hours," Dave pointed out, "and you've had almost one."

"Yeah, but I'm driving," Mark agreed, looking at the remnants of his beer. He'd left a good measure in the glass, and shrugged before tossing it back. "Maybe just half."

"Yeah yeah," Dave grumbled. "Scott?"

"No, I should head out," Scott replied.

"Okay then. Emma you want anything?" Dave pressed, still standing by the booth.

"No thanks," Emma said with a shake of her head.

"Your loss," Dave said. "I'll be right back."

"I should probably get going," Scott reiterated, more apologetic to Emma. "Thanks for having me."

"I'm glad you get along with Dave," Emma said with a smirk.

"I'm so glad you can argue his bullshit," Mark interrupted. "Dude has Opinions and we're not qualified to argue with him."

Scott laughed. "Yeah, it's kind of my day job, I'm used to it."

"Sorry," Emma added. "Wasn't expecting that to happen."

Scott shrugged. "It happens. What do I owe you for dinner?"

"You're not paying," Emma said, glaring at Scott.

"Why not?"

"Because you've got to run and you've been sitting here for three hours with us talking shit, and are probably late for whatever it is that you had to do. Besides, I invited you out unexpectedly. I'm buying your drink."

"Let me pitch in…"

"No," Emma insisted. "Get the hell outta here. I'll see you for the movie anyway, right?"

"Yeah," Scott agreed. "Thanks again."

"Anytime, dude," Mark said. "I think we'll just keep you around to temper Dave and his Opinions."

Scott laughed. "Yeah, okay." He flashed Emma another smile. "See you next week."

Emma nodded and kicked Mark under the table as she caught the knowing look he was giving her. "Shut up," she snapped.

"I'm not saying a damn word," Mark promised. "But you ought to keep him."

CHAPTER EIGHT

It seemed like time was crawling by since the night that they'd all gone out for drinks. Emma was a bundle of nerves and excitement by the time the movie night rolled around. Work had been keeping her busy, Mark had been gone and she'd not had a chance to go visit the comic shop - which wasn't a bad thing since she'd probably end up buying the trade issues that Scott was pushing on her. Avoiding the comic shop meant her wallet would be happy for another few days.

Mark stood in the doorway of the bathroom as Emma got ready to go out. He leaned casually against the doorframe, arms folded across his chest, head tilted as he watched her apply eye shadow.

"You've been standing there for like ten minutes," Emma said, staring at herself in the mirror.

"Yeah because this is weird."

"What's weird about this?" Emma asked. "You've known me for how long? You know that girls wear makeup."

"Why are you putting on makeup?" he asked after a long moment.

"War paint," Emma corrected with a smirk at herself in the mirror.

"Why are you putting on war paint?" Mark reiterated, changing his words but keeping the same flat tone. "You know we're going out to a movie, right?"

"Yes, I'm fully aware that we're going out to a movie, I was the one who set up this entire movie date night thing."

"So it's a date?" Mark asked, arching his eyebrow and grinning. He couldn't resist giving Emma good-natured ribbing whenever he could. They'd known each other for too long not to.

"No, it is not a date," Emma snapped. "Unless you and Luna are dating now?"

"Nope," Mark said easily. "That is definitely not a thing that's happening."

"Then it's a friendly group going out to a movie night."

"Date."

"Whatever, Mark," Emma said with a sigh and a shake of her head as she reached for the next colour for the palette she was applying to her eyelids. She was wearing her long black skirt, her favourite black sweater and a checkered sash around her waist. She'd opted for a sparkly silver and white eye shadow with black eye liner rather than the smoky eye she'd have usually done.

"So why are you applying war paint if it's just a friend thing?" Mark asked again, watching her choose her colours carefully.

"Because I don't get to go out very often and I want to look nice," Emma explained with an exasperated sigh. "I don't wear makeup at work 'cause kitchen plus makeup is a bad idea."

"You weren't wearing makeup when we went for drinks."

"I was wearing waterproof eyeliner," Emma corrected, eyeing Mark in the mirror. "I was at work before that, didn't want to go overboard. Like I said, kitchen plus makeup usually ends in a disaster."

"Yeah, I'm aware of that," Mark said, standing up straight as Emma leaned into the mirror to apply the silver eye shadow across her eyelids. "You like to point that out several times in any given conversation. But we're going to a movie. You're gonna either throw up from motion sickness or cry."

"I'm not going to cry," Emma argued.

"You cried at the last superhero movie we went to."

"That was emotional for me, okay?"

"You cried your way through the robots fighting kaiju movie."

Emma stopped and stared at Mark over her shoulder in the mirror. "And your point is?"

"You'd better make sure that you put waterproof eyeliner on over your sparkles,"

Mark teased with a grin. "And pack some extra tissues."

Emma sighed aloud, exaggerating the exhalation to make a point. "Why do you always have to ruin everything for me forever?"

"Hey, I'm not ruining anything," Mark said. "You're the one who always cries at everything because you're insane and over-emotional in the best of ways. I'm just reminding you that while it's very obvious that you're trying to impress your new friend, you probably don't want to look like a cross between a panda and a Goth metal reject when your mascara and eyeliner start running."

"You are so kind to always look out for me," Emma replied.

"I hear your sarcasm, and it is duly noted."

Emma laughed and shook her head. "Are you sure you don't want some Goth metal reject eyeliner?" She asked, waving the pencil at Mark.

"I'm all right, thanks," he assured her. "But you'd better hurry up or else we're going to be late, and I'm sure that you don't want to make that bad of an impression on your new friend."

"God," Emma said, rolling her eyes as she applied the finishing touches on her makeup. "Why do you have so say it so bitterly?"

"Because I say everything bitterly and with very little emotion?"

"Good point," Emma replied, turning her head to admire the makeup she'd put on. She nodded to herself; satisfied with the way she looked. "But why are you standing there watching me put on my makeup?"

"Because I find it utterly fascinating," Mark replied. "The lengths you girls will go through to impress someone. Besides, you wear makeup like once a month when you're not working. I think it's interesting to note which events merit your so-called war paint."

"So you're jealous and view me like a science experiment," Emma teased. "Got it. You ready to go?"

"Actually, I need to use the bathroom, but you've commandeered it for the last fifteen minutes."

Emma sighed again and shook her head. She put her makeup back in her case and set it on the shelf behind the door. She patted Mark's arm as she moved past him. "You know you could've just told me that in the first place."

"Naw, you were busy making yourself presentable. I can wait 'til you're done."

"Well hurry up," Emma said as she wandered to the front entrance to put on her shoes and coat. "We're running late!"

CHAPTER NINE

The theater was packed and crowds milled around in the lobby, waiting in line for snacks and tickets. Emma and Mark had arrived first and Emma stood in line to get tickets while Mark texted Luna to make sure she was still coming. They met up near the arcade by the doors.

"You wanna play a game while we wait?" Emma asked, handing Mark his ticket.

"God no," Mark replied. "Too many kids hovering around and the last time we tried, the machines ate our tokens, remember?"

"Oh yeah," Emma said with a nod. "I forgot."

"They don't keep up their machines worth a damn."

"So?" Emma asked, changing the subject. "What'd Luna say?"

"She's on her way, but might be a few minutes late so just save her a seat."

Emma sighed but nodded. "Does she want us to buy her a ticket?"

"No, she's good."

"Okay."

Mark draped his arm across Emma's shoulders. "You're way too tense for someone who's going to a movie."

"I am not," Emma replied with a scowl.

"You totally are," Mark argued, giving Emma a squeeze. "Why are you so nervous?"

"Crowds, mostly," Emma mumbled.

"Lies."

"Shut up."

"You want popcorn?" Mark asked.

"Yes. Is that even a question you need to ask?"

"Heh, good, 'cause I want candy."

"Here," Emma said, pulling cash out of her wallet. "I want caffeine, too."

"I love it when you shove money at me."

"I know," Emma teased. "It's better when I'm not just paying rent, right?"

"So much better," Mark agreed. "And the best part is that I get food out of this, too."

Emma laughed and shooed Mark on with a wave of her hand. She was getting nervous because it was getting late and the movie was supposed to start just after seven. She hadn't heard from Scott, and she hoped that he was still going to join them. The lobby was crowded and Emma watched the people coming in carefully, looking for Scott. She was short and easy to miss, so she kept a careful eye out for the familiar face.

She didn't have to wait long before she spotted him walking through the doors. Somehow, he managed to find her quickly and he waved and pointed to the ticket line. She nodded and he went to grab his ticket. Emma waited for him on the other side of the line-up. She threw her arms open and he took the invitation.

"Hey! I was afraid you weren't going to make it."

"I said seven, didn't I?" Scott replied, breaking the hug first.

"You look damn good," Emma said, looking him over appraisingly. He was dressed up, wearing a suit with his hair slicked back. "You look mildly evil, I dig it. You okay?"

"Thanks." Scott said easily. "Yes, I'm fine, stuff had to happen today that required a suit. Don't ask, it's a long story."

"This is definitely your super villain origin story, isn't it?"

"Ha, no. Maybe. Doubt it. I was just, you know, supporting a friend."

"In court?"

"You wish."

"You could pull of the Matt Murdock in that suit."

Scott grinned. "I might have the right glasses for that."

"Oh my," Emma replied, faking a swoon and fanning herself with her hand. "You've just become the most attractive person in the room."

"Just now? I mean, I thought I was already there. But you got a thing for blind boys?"

"No, Catholics with superpowers."

"Oh, well, I probably shouldn't tell you about my childhood, or about all those secret powers, like my super speed, or my vast intelligence verging on psychic abilities."

Emma laughed. "Yeah, you're definitely evil."

"I'm starving," Scott interrupted, changing the subject. "I'm gonna grab food, you want anything?"

"Mark is somewhere in line getting popcorn for me," Emma replied. "Go."

Scott disappeared into the crowd to grab dinner while Emma waited for everyone to get back. Luna still hadn't showed up, and Emma was worried. She pulled out her phone and sent her a quick text saying they'd meet her in the theater, and they'd save her a seat.

Scott and Mark returned at the same time. Scott had acquired pizza, and Mark held out the popcorn Emma had requested and she eyed it incredulously.

"That's a lot of popcorn," Emma said. "And you don't like popcorn.

Mark shrugged. "I'm sure you'll figure something out."

Emma shook her head and took the bag from Mark. "Haven't heard from Luna, sent her a text though. Said we'd save her a seat."

"Okie dokie," Mark agreed. "We'd better hurry up and go find seats, then. It's pretty busy in here."

Emma saluted with her free hand and followed Mark, with Scott walking along beside her.

"Who's Luna?" Scott asked.

"Other friend I've known almost as long as Mark," Emma replied. "She's fun. Relax."

"I'm perfectly relaxed," Scott grumbled as they handed over their tickets to be torn.

"You're dressed up," Emma pointed out. "In a suit. How relaxed can you possibly be?"

"All the best villains wear suits," Scott replied. "And they're always calm and collected."

"You're a basket case," Mark said as they found seats. "You do know that, right?"

"I'm glad it's that apparent," Scott agreed, taking a seat between Emma and Mark. He leaned forward to get Emma's attention as she set her coat and bag on the floor by her feet. "Hey."

"What?" Emma asked, giving Scott a sideways glance.

"Now I can get fresh with both of you," Scott said, with a lecherous grin.

"Aww yeah," Mark added, placing his hand on Scott's knee.

Emma leaned forward and pointed an accusatory finger at Mark. "Keep your hands off of him, he's mine," she warned, earning a laugh from both of her boys.

"You brought new people?" Luna asked as she stopped next to Emma, who was sitting on the edge of the row.

"Luna!" Emma exclaimed, standing to throw her arms around her friend. "You made it!"

"Barely," Luna agreed, peering around Emma to stare at Scott. "New person."

Scott waved with his free hand, his mouth full of pizza.

"That's Scott," Emma said, giving Luna a knowing look.

"Oh," Luna said with a grin. "I see. He actually does exist."

"I don't, I promise," Scott replied. "I presume you're Luna?"

"She warned you about me, didn't she?" Luna replied as she scooted past Scott to take a seat next to Mark. "That's no good."

"She's not that bad," Mark interrupted, throwing his arm over Luna's shoulder in an awkward hug. "We wouldn't have kept her this long if she was."

"You guys have super low standards," Luna whispered.

"Was I not supposed to hear that?" Scott asked with a laugh.

"We have excellent standards, thank you," Mark argued. "We just tend to keep hold of the people who fit those standards and not let go. And then, eventually, you drink the Kool-Aid."

Scott fixed Emma with a look that said 'I told you so'.

"I'm not a serial killer, I swear," Emma said. "Luna wouldn't still be sitting here if I were."

"That's true, she's not," Luna agreed. "The last two roommates were totally accidental."

"I need to leave," Scott said quickly, making like he needed to get up. Emma placed a hand on his leg and Mark did the same to his shoulder.

"You're not going anywhere," Mark whispered in a vaguely threatening manner, causing Emma to dissolve into a fit of giggles.

You guys are so screwed up," Scott said.

"You love it," Emma replied.

"Love isn't the word I'd use, but since we're lacking any other emotions, sure."

"Careful, Emma," Mark teased. "If you tell him too much, we might have to kill him."

Emma sighed. "Or we kill you and he replaces you."

"Isn't that the plot of --"

"Don't you dare start talking comics," Emma warned. "No comics talk tonight."

"I wasn't even gonna mention that secret takeover the alien invasion caused in comics," Mark promised.

Scott groaned under his breath. "I hate you."

"We all hate him, too," Luna joked. "We just needed a muscleman in the girl gang."

"So maybe we *should* kill him and let Scott replace him?"

"Is Scott any better at keeping secrets?" Luna asked.

"He might be a cannibal, so I assume yes."

Scott nodded.

"We'll decide after the movie," Luna said. "Since the lights are going down and I don't feel like murdering Mark right now."

"That's a fair point," Emma said.

"Congratulations," Scott interrupted. "You get to live through this movie."

"I'm not worried," Mark assured Scott. "She'd have to go through you to get to me, and also, I pay half the rent."

"Money is a very good motivator," Scott agreed.

The conversation died out as the movie started Emma held out the popcorn to Scott once he was finished his pizza, and he accepted. Eventually, Emma just handed him the whole bag.

"God I don't want any more popcorn," Emma mumbled.

Scott laughed. "Sissy."

"I'm gonna die."

"Over popcorn?"

"And how *bored* I am."

"Not enjoying the movie?"

"It's all *Pride and Prejudice* and not enough vampires."

"Who are the vampires?"

"Well… I thought it was those two, but they're in the sun so…"

"You actually have no idea what this movie is supposed to be, do you?"

"It's Victorian costume porn, is what it is," Emma whispered.

"Edwardian," Scott corrected.

"Fucking *nerd*," Emma teased.

"It's not Victorian, trust me."

"Same shit -- "

"It's so not."

"-- Different repressions," Emma concluded.

Scott chuckled. "I don't… I don't even know how to argue that."

"Just watch the damn movie," Emma suggested.

They fell into silence for a long while, watching the movie and not making the sarcastic comments they both wanted to. Emma caught Scott's eye more than once, and she pressed a finger to her lips, stopping any more comments.

"Oh shit, ghosts!" Scott whispered suddenly, catching Emma off guard and causing her to laugh.

"You ass."

"Everyone is dead."

"It's a premonition," Emma hissed back. "Shut up."

"Everyone is dead and the ghosts are gonna getcha."

"Yes, that's exactly what's going on."

"You're not even paying attention."

"I'm pretty motion sick, to be honest," Emma admitted.

"Well, everyone is dead, and now they're going to some obscure place to do obscure things and there might be ghosts in the new place."

"Is that it?"

"And the blonde guy is mad at the dark-haired guy for stealing the girl, and the other girl is actually Satan."

"Okay, got it," Emma said with a sigh, falling back into comfortable silence.

"They're gonna have the sex," Scott whispered suddenly.

Emma coughed a laugh into her hand, trying not to crack up loudly in the theater as she hissed back, "Hey, at least they're married."

"You're such a prude," Scott teased.

Emma sighed in exasperation. "No, this movie is the prude. That was the most Victorian…"

"Edwardian," Scott corrected.

"Victorian," Emma continued, unperturbed, "sex scene I have ever seen. That was literally in the trailer. I'm so done with this movie."

"Because of the sex scene?"

"Because while this is the prettiest Jane Austen fan fiction I have ever had the pleasure of watching, I have absolutely no clue what's going on."

"Those two are having sex," Scott offered. "And now that one is mad at them, and the ghosts are watching everything."

"Yes, thank you," Emma replied, burying her face in her hands. As the movie droned on, the banter between Emma and Scott stalled as the action built up and plot points were revealed.

"Oh shit, it's more ghosts," Scott muttered.

Emma chuckled and leaned her head against his shoulder. "But where's the doctor guy?"

"He's busy pretending to be Sherlock Holmes back in London."

"Okay, but… Wait… this isn't happening, is it?" Emma asked, suddenly very tense.

"Oh, something bad is happening," Scott teased.

"Lullabies in movies are never a good sign…" Emma whined.

"Do you need to cover your eyes?" Scott asked.

"I might," Emma whined.

"Sissy."

"Shh. That's my secret."

"At least it's not that you're in love with a ghost."

"Oh noooooo…." Emma groaned as the movie plot picked up in intensity. "Why does she have a knife?"

"Why doesn't *everyone* have a knife?"

Emma jolted in her seat and covered her face with her hands as one character stabbed another in the face. "Oh, God why?" she said, much louder than she intended, causing Scott to crack up.

"Are you really gonna puke?" Scott asked as Emma leaned forward.

"Maybe," she complained. "Why would they do that?"

"Specifically to make you puke."

"I hate this movie."

Scott laughed. "Everyone is a ghost now."

Emma made a whining noise and leaned back in her seat, frowning and fell silent again as the movie reached the end. She was leaning against Scott's shoulder as the credits rolled and she didn't move right away. He reached over and patted her head.

"You didn't puke," he said. "I'm impressed."

"Stop patting my head," Emma whined.

"No. These are comforting pats. You're now feeling comforted."

Emma whined and sat up, shoving Scott's hand away and leaning forward to look over at Luna and Mark. "What'd you guys think?"

"That was most definitely a movie with a sex scene in it," Mark said.

"That wasn't the scariest thing I've ever seen," Luna added. "And now I'm kinda depressed."

"It was a depressing movie. We need ice cream therapy," Emma said.

"Yes, we do," Luna agreed. "Where?"

"Diner across the street?" Emma suggested. "They have ice cream." She looked at Scott. "You okay with that?"

"Yes I am," Scott agreed.

They got up and headed out of the theatre, Emma and Luna talking about life stuff that Mark and Scott weren't privy to as they headed toward the diner in question. The hostess led them to the booth and Scott and Emma slid into one side, while Luna and Mark took the other side. Luna sat directly across from Emma.

"Pie," Luna said.

"No ice cream?"

"Ice cream on the side."

Emma laughed. "Wanna share?"

"More pie is always good."

The waiter arrived to take their orders and Emma and Luna ordered a slice of each pie on the menu, with a single scoop of ice cream on the side.

"Are you two dating?" Scott asked.

"Yes," Emma and Luna deadpanned together.

"Why does everyone always ask that?" Luna asked.

Emma shrugged. "I think it's 'cause we're just so cuddly."

"Or everyone forever is a freak who has never seen a healthy platonic relationship between two women that wasn't completely fetishized by media."

"Oh God, is she like Dave?" Scott asked, grabbing Emma's arm.

Emma and Luna both started laughing.

"Oh Lord, no," Luna promised. "That's about as smart as I get. I get one per week."

"So you're saying that I shouldn't be fetishizing you two?"

"I'm not wearing the right mail order outfit for that," Luna agreed, arching an eyebrow and giving Scott a look that suggested she could kill him with a thought.

"You want me to stab him under the table?" Emma asked.

"Would you?"

"For you? Absolutely." Emma picked up her butter knife and poked Scott in the leg, just hard enough to give him a warning.

"What the hell?" Scott whined, shoving Emma's hand away.

"You really do lack conviction don't you?" Emma teased. "Hard to cope with someone who doesn't, isn't it?"

"You're insane."

"Ten percent," Emma agreed. "I think Luna adds two percent though."

"I have to go," Scott deadpanned.

Emma poked him in the leg again.

"Rude, holy shit," Scott said, shoving Emma's hand away again to the delight of the others, causing them to laugh as their desserts were brought to the table.

"Why don't you ever talk, Mark?" Scott asked.

"Because when you hang around these two," he gestured toward Emma and Luna, "there is very little need for you to talk."

"I'm gonna stab you, too," Emma warned.

"Then you can walk home," Mark replied with a smirk as Luna helped herself to pie across the table.

"I'll drive you if you stab him," Luna offered.

"See why I never talk?" Mark joked. "You can't ever win with them."

"Maybe we should date," Emma suggested.

"I would love to date you," Luna replied, "but you're not my type."

"Oh right, I always forget that we're both girls."

Scott patted Emma's head in fake condolences, and she held up her butter knife again.

"Your pie looks terrible," Scott said.

"It's not very good," Emma agreed.

"That's like mostly gelatin."

"It's… yeah," Emma complained

"Mmm, cow part pie."

"Do you want some?" Emma asked, putting a piece on her fork and threatening to shove it in Scott's face.

"No! God, ew. I don't know where you've been!"

"That's a very good point," Emma agreed.

"She doesn't go anywhere or do anything," Luna said. "So you can assume that she's relatively clean and disease-free."

"I'm non-GMO."

"But not free range or organic," Mark added.

"I actually don't want this pie," Emma said, scraping the supposedly gelatin-filled pie off her fork and back onto the plate.

"Yeah, this was a bad idea," Luna agreed. "Sorry."

Emma shrugged. "It's been fun though."

"It has," Scott agreed. "I should probably start heading back though."

"Yeah, me too," Luna said. "I have work tomorrow."

They asked for their bills and Emma paid for Luna's pie before they headed out into the dark.

"Where'd you park?" Emma asked Mark.

"Back by the theater," Mark replied. "Did you forget?"

"Yes…"

Luna laughed. "I did, too, it's fine."

"What about you, Scott?"

"I'm taking the bus, it's all good."

"You wanna ride?" Mark offered.

113

"Nope. I'm fine."

"Okay," Mark said, wrapping his arms around him in a bear hug.

"Oh, Mark, you're so muscular and strong," Scott swooned sarcastically.

"You should check out my ass," Mark replied.

Scott reached over and grabbed Mark's ass without hesitation. He made a small noise of approval. "Not bad."

"What?" Mark asked is yours better?

"I bike everywhere, it damn well better be," Scott replied.

Mark took it as an invitation and gave Scott a quick grope. "Yeah, okay, yours is pretty good, too."

"Quit molesting each other, oh my *God*," Emma said, throwing her hands up in exasperation.

"You love it," Scott teased, draping his arm around Emma's shoulders and pulling her close. She was just the perfect height to tuck under his arm, so she wrapped her arm tentatively around his waist.

"Nope," Emma replied as he squeezed her shoulders quickly before letting her go. "Get home safely."

"See you for comics," Scott said quietly before waving and taking off toward the bus stop.

Emma scowled at his retreating shape. "Ass."

"It is a nice one," Mark confirmed.

Emma scowled at Mark. "Quit manhandling my plaything," she warned.

Luna and Mark exchanged looks and started to laugh before draping their arms collectively over Emma's shoulders and leading her back to the cinema parking lot.

CHAPTER TEN

"Funny how we're always meeting up like this." Emma said with a smirk as she walked to the till carrying her pile of comics the next Wednesday.

"You'd almost think I work here," Scott replied. "And that you come in and buy comics every week."

"Seems like that, yeah."

"Why don't you set up a pull list?" Scott asked as he eyed her choices. "Then I just have to get them out of your file, and you won't miss anything."

"Well I have a friend who keeps track of this for me, I always just ask Ian what's coming out this week…"

"You treat your friend like a walking Previews magazine?" Scott asked with an air of scandal in his voice. "How could you possibly do that to another person?"

"What do you mean how could I treat another person like that?"

"Have you ever actually looked at a copy of Previews?"

"Yes," Emma said. "I don't have the patience for it. Besides, Ian is really good at keeping track of release dates, and he reads more comics than I do. We talk a lot, so I don't have to remember what's coming out. And, you know, he does it anyway, so I just take advantage of his knowledge and use it whenever I can."

Scott smirked as he flipped through her stack of books. "Okay, but you're missing that one about the pop idol gods."

"That's out this week?"

"Yeah. See what I mean?"

Emma sighed and wandered back through the store to the new releases section, scanning the shelves until she found the wayward issue she was missing.

"How did you miss that one?" Scott asked as Emma set it on the pile with her other books. "It's bright pink."

"Have you seen the new releases this week?" she countered. "There's at least three of them with bright pink covers and I kinda wanna throw up."

"What? You're not a fan of neon pink?"

"Not really," Emma said. "I like pink, it's part of my bedroom colour scheme, but not like 80's nostalgia burn your eyes out pink."

"But you're ruining a perfectly good stereotype!"

Emma laughed. "Yeah, I know, I'm totally the target demographic for some of those books. The gender-swapped alternate reality where the superhero dude is a girl? I know that I *should* love it based on the marketing but I picked it up, flipped through it and just went no thanks."

"Because it sucks?"

"Because… I don't know. I just didn't care for it overall?"

"Maybe I was wrong and you have less crappy taste in comics than I thought."

Emma laughed. "Maybe I'm just not as easily defined by a target demographic as most marketing executives would think I am, and therefore am an outlier and should probably be burned at the stake for witchcraft?"

"You must love the scantily-clad heroes then."

"Which ones?"

"All of them?" Scott suggested.

Emma nodded. "Oh yes, the more scantily clad and impractical the costume, the better. Sign me up for battle bikinis and capes."

"I'm not entirely sure that you're supposed to agree with me on that sort of stuff."

"Why not?" Emma asked. "Does it ruin your elitist attitude and make you feel awkward when someone of the fairer sex is actually on your side for once?"

"Something like that," Scott agreed with a grin.

"Am I weirding you out?" Emma asked.

"I don't know."

"I don't think you're allowed to be weirded out by anything I say anymore," Emma pointed out. "At least not about me agreeing with the sexy scantily clad women in comics. And how there needs to be more sexy men and less clothes on them in comics, too."

"I'm not allowed to be weirded out by this?"

"Nope," Emma agreed. "For one, why is that weird?"

Scott shrugged. "Usually I get complaints about the skin tight costumes and lack of tact that female comic characters have?"

Emma rolled her eyes. "Oh well, then, yeah, I can see why you'd be weirded out when someone like me ruins stereotypes and actually actively looks for battle bikinis."

"Do you own a battle bikini?"

"That's classified," Emma said with a firm nod.

"So that's a no."

"That's a shut your damn mouth."

Scott laughed. "You're so mean."

"Only when I'm in a good mood."

Scott shook his head. "That's fine, I can deal with you being mean. It's not like I have feelings anyway. You do anything interesting this week?" He rambled, effortlessly changing the subject." Go out anywhere fun?"

"Not since the movie the other night."

"That was the worst movie I've seen in a long time."

"You weren't the one retching at the end of it."

Scott laughed. "Oh right when that one guy got stabbed in the face!"

"No!" Emma whined.

"And then the knife was stuck right there," he added, pointing to the spot just under his eye where the character in question had been stabbed. "The *best* part about that was the silence that followed, when he was pulling the knife out of his face and you could hear the metal scraping. Against. The. Bone."

Emma shuddered and made a gagging noise. "I hate you."

Scott's grin was filled with a sort of malicious glee as he poorly imitated the sound of metal scraping against bone. "I mean, that was an impressive stab wound, she'd have to have broken through his damn skull…"

"Okay! Enough!" Emma whined. "I'm so sorry for giving you shit today."

"Still so sarcastic."

Emma pouted, giving Scott the best injured puppy look that she could muster

"You do know that you shouted 'oh God, why?' in the theater, right?"

"Did I embarrass you?" Emma asked.

"Pfft, no. I'm plenty good at embarrassing myself, and shouting uncontrollably at the movie is probably the least embarrassing thing to have happened to me this week."

"Oh, that's something that I need you to elaborate on," Emma said with a laugh. "Desperately need you to elaborate on that one."

"So you're getting *Sam Wilson: Captain America* today, right?" Scott replied, changing the subject. "I'll go grab it off the shelf for you and everything."

"No," she replied with another low chuckle. "Why do you keep pushing that one?"

"Because it's *amazing* and made so many people angry."

Emma shrugged and wrinkled her nose. "I'm not into politically charged, angry comics, man."

"I rescind my opinion of your taste in comics."

"I don't need you to approve of my taste in comics," Emma replied matter-of-factly. "I'm so far beyond giving a shit what anyone thinks about what I like."

"Fair enough," Scott said, presenting Emma with a piece of paper.

"What's that?"

"Your pull list," Scott replied. "Just write down what series you want to keep up with, and then you get a number and you come in every week and your stuff is ready. All we ask is that you come pick up your comics at least once every two weeks."

"And what if I hate something on this list after three issues?" Emma asked, eyeing the blank form warily. "I mean, I've dropped like six series already because I got bored or hated the art or whatever."

Scott shrugged. "You tell me and I take it off your pull list. It's not a big deal."

"Okay fine," Emma sighed. Scott grinned widely and handed her a pen. "I can't believe you're convincing me to do this."

"Next you should totally go buy the Waid run of Daredevil."

"Shut up," Emma complained. "That's not happening."

"We have the first five trades in stock *right now*."

"No."

"I'll go grab them for you while you decide what you want to add to your pull list."

"No."

"Are you absolutely sure?"

"Are you going to give me a discount if I buy them?" Emma asked without looking up from the list she was making.

"That's not a thing that happens here."

"Then, no, I'm good. I'll just read them online."

"That's stealing," Scott warned. "I dunno if we can be friends."

"I have a subscription to the unlimited comic streaming thing," Emma replied, clicking the pen and offering it back to Scott. "I'll go log in and read them. Or maybe, I'll just ask my walking Previews magazine if he's got them on digital, I'm sure he'll give me his password and let me borrow his account."

"You're getting all kinds of excited about semi-legal piracy today, aren't you?"

"You learn to beg and borrow when you don't have access to the stuff you want," Emma replied with a nonchalant shrug.

"You didn't put Sam Wilson on your pull list," Scott pointed out. "I'll just fix that for you."

Emma reached over the counter and snatched the pen from Scott's hand. "I'll kill you with this pen," she warned.

"I'd be impressed," Scott admitted. "I don't think I've ever been threatened with a pen."

"You'll get used to it," Emma replied, handing the pen back.

Scott laughed. "Okay, so… give me a second, I'll go get your box number and set this up for you. Two seconds."

Emma fidgeted in her spot by the counter as Scott disappeared behind the partition wall where the pull list files were kept. She wanted to ask him something, but she was nervous. It didn't take him long to come back and he handed Emma a card.

"So this has got your box number on it, so just remind me what it is when you come to get your comics. You'll get an email every week, too, so you'll always know what's out."

Emma nodded. "This is the first time I've ever had one of these set up."

"Really?" Scott asked. "And you've been reading comics for how long?"

"Long enough," she replied. "Just never really had the desire to stay that connected I guess. And I go in bursts. I'll drop everything once I get bored, so it never really seemed necessary for me to bother with having a weekly pull list set up."

"Congratulations," Scott said. "You're officially a geek now."

"Still more of a geek than you are."

"I make an excellent fake geek girl," he agreed.

Emma chuckled and shook her head. She needed to ask him the question that she'd been dying to ask for weeks, and she still didn't know how. She took a breath and just blurted out, "Wouldn't it be better to go hang out elsewhere?"

"Elsewhere?" Scott asked. "Like the movies?"

"Maybe not the movies," Emma replied slowly.

"Yeah, I'm up for that," Scott agreed with a shrug. "What were you thinking?"

Emma shrugged. "Dinner after work one night?" she suggested. "I mean, you're not actually a robot or something, right? I assume you eat?"

"I am a sad robot," Scott corrected.

"No, your aesthetic is sad robots," Emma argued, earning a laugh.

"My aesthetic," Scott muttered, shaking his head, and still laughing. "Yeah, that's exactly it. I love sad robots."

"Sad robots just generally require love," Emma agreed. "Just give 'em all hugs."

"I am looking forward to the sad robot comic."

"I added that one to the pull list, just so you wouldn't give me shit over it," Emma said.

"Good," Scott replied. "Then yeah, we can go hang out somewhere else."

Emma huffed. "Excuse me? Are you saying that you'd not have agreed to go hang out with me if my pull list didn't meet your standards?"

"Not at all," Scott replied.

"Your sarcasm is showing again."

"I'm not being sarcastic!" Scott insisted. "I just like sad robots and if you're not going to read Sam Wilson, then the least you can do is listen to my advice and read the sad robots."

125

Emma pinched the bridge of her nose and groaned into her hand. "You're infuriating, you know that, right?"

"Yeah, I do," Scott agreed, beaming with misplaced pride. "So this elsewhere hanging out? Where's this happening?"

Emma shrugged. "Dinner?"

"After work," Scott agreed.

"I'll come down here, if you want?"

"Probably easiest."

"Next Wednesday?"

"Sure. We close at six."

"I *know*," Emma breathed. "It's not like I'm here every week or anything."

"I know, it's weird," Scott deadpanned as the doorbell rang and a few people entered the store. "I've never seen you before."

"Shut up," Emma laughed. "I'll see you next week."

"Yeah," Scott replied. "You'll have to pick up your comics."

"You're such an ass."

Scott laughed as Emma picked up her bag from its spot on the floor. "And then," he added, "I'll see you for dinner, too."

CHAPTER ELEVEN

They'd agreed to meet up after work. Emma arrived early; she had comics to pick up, after all. The weather had been mild, and she'd dressed up as much as she could for it being the middle of winter. Her dress caught in the wind as she walked to the store and she cursed as she walked, thankful that she'd worn leggings and boots, but still annoyed by the fact that the wind had picked up, dropping the temperature as much as it had and threatening snow.

Scott wasn't behind the till when she walked in and she felt a momentary panic hit her. He hadn't called to cancel,

She walked past the till, looking for new releases that she hadn't put on her list as the other cashier went to get list. She frowned to herself, Scott was nowhere in sight. She browsed the wall of comics, nothing was catching her eye.

"Don't forget this one."

Scott had appeared and was holding out a single issue. "You're still reading this one, right?'

Emma nodded and took the proffered comic. "I was debating on the toys," she added, nodding toward a couple of action figures on the shelf next to the comics. "I like the bad guys."

"I'd say get them, but apparently I'm no good at convincing you to buy anything, since you're still not reading Daredevil."

"There's a very big difference in a ten dollar action figure and a twenty five dollar book."

Scott shrugged. "I suppose."

"Besides, I'll stage an epic battle on my desk, including an elaborate trap made out of sharpened pencils."

"You have too much spare time on your hands."

"I have exactly enough spare time on my hands to set up an elaborate trap made out of sharpened pencils for a ten dollar action figure," Emma corrected.

"Still seems like more than a usual amount of spare time," Scott said with a shrug.

Emma frowned and shrugged. "Guess so. Better that I don't get the action figure, then, isn't it?" She sighed. "We're still on for tonight, right?" she asked. He was being blunt and less friendly than usual.

Scott nodded. "Yeah."

"I'll meet you over at the coffee place, then?"

"Sounds good," Scott agreed. "See you in a bit."

Emma smiled and went to pay for her purchases before heading over to the coffee shop. Her favourite barista was working behind the register and she smiled brightly when she saw him.

"Hey!" he exclaimed. "I haven't seen you in forever."

"Did you switch your shifts?"

"Temporarily, yeah."

"Ah," Emma said with a nod. "Explains why I haven't seen you in a long time."

"Sorry, didn't mean to scare you."

Emma laughed. "I haven't been drinking coffee, so it's probably a better thing for me. Less caffeine in tea than espresso."

"So are you having tea then?"

"No, you're here. I want a coffee. Vanilla latte."

"You got it," the blond barista said with a grin. "I'm glad you're still around."

"Really?"

"Yeah, you're fun to talk to."

"Aww, thanks, so what have you been up to?" Emma asked as she paid for her $5 coffee.

"School, mostly."

"High school?"

"Yeah, I graduate in a couple months and I can't tell you haw excited I am."

Emma grinned. "I can imagine. Got plans for after?"

"Not really," the barista said, moving over to make Emma's drink. "I don't know exactly what I want to do."

"Nothing wring with that," Emma replied. "I'm glad you're doing well though."

"Yeah, I'm happy to see you, too." He smiled and handed Emma her cup, before nodding toward her usual spot. "It's been empty all day."

Emma looked over her shoulder to her favourite booth in the corner by the window and laughed. "Well, I'm going to go and take it over for a little while," she said. "Thank you very much."

"You're welcome."

Emma settled into her usual spot in the corner with a happy sigh, sipping on her coffee as she flipped through her weekly comics. It felt like all of the stories were in a transition, changing story lines as arcs all came to an end all at the same time. She finished reading all of her comics and put them into her bag before pulling out her phone to check the time. It was just before six. She still had twenty minutes to kill before Scott would come to join her. She felt her stomach flip in excited nervousness and was suddenly very aware that she'd been out almost all day and she hadn't eaten. She sipped her coffee slower, hoping the milk would settle her stomach a little, rather than make her feel worse. She scrolled through her phone, flipping between social media apps and games while she waited, but nothing really kept her attention for very long.

Finally, she put her phone away and looked out the window. A very familiar shape was walking through the dark toward the coffee shop. Emma couldn't help but smile as Scott hurried across the street. Although, Emma reconsidered, hurrying to her was probably closer to his normal speed.

Stupid long legged jerk.

Emma grinned to herself as she put her phone back in her bag and made sure that all of her belongings were tucked away. Scott was distracting, she wouldn't be surprised if she forgot something while they were visiting, better to put everything away now.

"You always sit here, don't you?" Scott asked as he approached.

"If I can, yeah," Emma replied with a smile.

"I could see you in the window," he pointed out.

"I could see you, too. That's kind of what windows *do*, Scott."

"I meant… Never mind."

Emma laughed. "Okay, sorry."

"You're not wearing a black sweater," Scott added with a shrug. "It's different."

"Oh, yeah, I just… didn't want to wear the black one I guess. Um…" She hesitated. "Are you okay?"

"Yeah, I'm fine. Why?"

"You seemed… not happy?"

"Oh, no sorry, everything is okay," Scott said. "I mean, it was stupid busy today and I didn't have a chance to eat or really leave the till today. I spent three goddamn hours filling shelves and it was just not a good day."

"That sucks," Emma said offering an apologetic grin. "To be fair, I kind of forgot to eat today, too."

"We are *so good* at being adults."

"I'm surprised I haven't just died from lack of sleep and over-caffeinating yet."

Scott nodded. "Yeah, that's about where I am. Told you, who needs food?"

"Well considering that neither of us has eaten at all today…"

"Shh," Scott hissed with a grin.

"I'm glad you're in a better mood now that you're out of the store," Emma said, standing to put on her coat. "But we should probably go acquire a meal somewhere before we both go into hypoglycemic shock."

"That sounds like a very good plan."

They walked out into the dark, chilly, not-quite-winter air and Emma shoved her hands into her coat pockets, trying desperately to keep herself warm against the wind.

"So, where do you want to go?"

Scott made a noncommittal noise and shrugged. "Same place we went for drinks last time?"

"That sounds like a plan," Emma agreed with a nod.

"Except not pizza this time."

Emma laughed. "Yeah, we fed you like a whole pizza didn't we?"

"Damn near," Scott agreed. "Your friends are weird."

"Yeah, but that's why they're my friends."

"Good point." He hesitated. "I'm definitely nowhere near that weird though."

"No, you're my kind of straight up evil, though."

Scott narrowed his eyes. "Is that a good thing?"

"It can be," Emma said. "It means that I can at least ask you to be my alibi when I inevitably snap and murder someone."

"Okay. I can do that, but I'm not helping you bury the body."

"Bury? Please," Emma scoffed. "Quicklime is so much easier."

"Lye in the bathtub," Scott suggested.

"Eh, I live in a rental house. I don't really think that my landlord would be too happy if I gum up the plumbing with dead guy slurry. Plus, I have a roommate."

133

"That is a problem," Scott agreed as they reached the bar. He opened the door and held it for Emma.

Inside the bar was warm and dark, the way all good, modern bars ought to be. The lights weren't turned up, but the music certainly was. Emma led the way through the familiar bar to the same booth they'd occupied when they'd gone drinking with Mark and Dave. Emma slid into the middle of the booth, draping her coat over the single chair before she did, and tucking her bag next to her. Scott followed, sitting close, but not as close as they'd been in the small booth at the diner after the movie.

"You sure you don't want pizza?" Emma teased as the waitress came to take their drink order.

"I am sure that I don't want pizza," Scott replied, looking over the menu. "But I'll have a Coke to start."

"Diet for me," Emma added to the waitress.

"Sounds good," the waitress said with a smile. "I'll be right back."

Emma glanced up at the television, reading the ticker tape scrolling over the bottom of the screen.

"That's sportsball," Scott said. "National pastime of drunken rednecks."

"You sure that's not lacrosse?" Emma joked. It was hockey.

134

"No, that's sportsball," Scott confirmed. "The point is to get the football across the pitch and do as much physical damage to the other players with the beating sticks as possible. That's the Quidditch stopper and he's supposed to try to keep the disk-ball out of the goal."

Emma buried her face in her hands, giggling and shaking her head. "What the hell is wrong with you?"

"I'm just explaining sportsball to you," Scott replied, "Don't you know how to *sports*?"

"I have not had enough caffeine for this," Emma muttered, taking a sip of her Coke. "Or perhaps I've had too much and I've looped back around to feeling like death."

"I've had too much, it's awesome," Scott replied. "I can feel it in my *eyes*."

"I still think you're better off than I am tonight."

"It's the caffeine," Scott confirmed.

Their waitress walked over to the table then. "Are you guys ready to order?"

"Oh God, I forgot that food is a thing we need…" Emma said.

"Hey, mozza sticks," Scott said, glancing at the menu.

"Oh God…" Emma replied.

"Can we start with that and then give us a minute?"

The waitress laughed and nodded. "Sure, I'll ring that in."

135

Emma gave Scott a sideways look. "Really?"

Scott smiled widely. "Yes, really."

"Delicious."

"You look super less than enthused about this."

"I am super less than enthused," Emma agreed. "This being an adult business is hard."

"We are both totally good at being adults. Not eating and then feeling like you're gonna die? Awesome. That's adulthood in a nutshell."

Emma rested her head against her hand, elbow on the table as she stared incredulously at Scott. She couldn't help but smile, and his ridiculousness had elevated her mood. She was a lot less nervous now; it was nice to be out of the comic shop, and away from everyone else.

"So?" Scott asked.

"So, what?"

Scott shrugged. "Anything fabulously interesting going on in your life?"

"Work and work and work," Emma replied. "Staying with my mom this week while painters are in my house."

"That sucks."

"What does?"

"Having painters in your house. I hate having people in my space."

"Yeah, I get it," Emma agreed. "Whatcha gonna do? Landlord decided that the house needs paint. What about you?"

"Work is my all, ever-consuming reason for existing."

"At least you can afford all your comics."

Scott groaned. "Oh, God, I forgot how many I have this week."

"That many?"

"Too many."

"You could always --"

"Don't even suggest it," Scott interrupted. "I can't stop reading them."

"You can, you just won't."

"How else am I going to tell everyone which comics they need to buy?"

"Well, you can just suggest stuff based off of online reviews and save the seven million dollars you spend on comics. Besides, no one ever takes your suggestions anyway."

Scott shook his head. "You're evil and rude and that hurts my feelings."

"You have feelings?"

"I have some… maybe."

"Caffeination is not a feeling," Emma replied. "It's a state of being."

Scott laughed and the waitress returned with the order of mozzarella sticks Scott had requested. Emma tried not to wince at the plate as the waitress set it between them. The idea of eating was unappealing, even though she knew she hadn't eaten enough for the day, and deep fried pub food was not what she wanted.

"I'll come back in a few minutes to get your main order?"

"Sure, thanks," Emma said with a nod.

"Mmm, deep fried cheese," Scott said, eyeing the plate with a look of confusion. "Why the hell is it served with ranch dip?"

Emma shook her head. "I have no idea, but that seems really gross."

Scott dipped the first mozza stick in the ranch and took a bite. He shrugged. "Could be worse."

Emma winced and shook her head. "Gross."

"What?"

"Just, mozza sticks."

"You don't like them?"

"I usually wouldn't say no, but… I just…"

"Come on," Scott said picking up another one and dipping it in ranch. He held it out to Emma, waving it in her face. "Come on, you know you wanna."

"Oh my God," Emma snapped, laughing. "Are you *trying* to seduce me?"

"Put my mozza stick in your mouth."

"Ew!" Emma slapped his hand away. "Get that shit out of my face. I swear, I will throw up if I put that in my mouth."

"Are *you* trying to seduce me?" Scott replied. "I bet you say that to all the boys, don't you?"

"Only the ones who have no idea what they're doing."

"And you assume I don't know?"

"You're a boy, aren't you?"

Scott laughed and stared at Emma. He held eye contact for a long moment, before licking the ranch off the end of the mozza stick and taking a bite. Emma made a gagging noise as Scott cracked up, eyes darting past her as people walked past the big window.

"Did you see those girls walking past the window as I just did that?"

"Yeah?"

Scott shook his head. "I accidentally made eye contact with one of them."

"Oh, so that's why they sped up?"

Scott shrugged and took another mozza stick. "Apparently. I hope they weren't planning on coming in here."

"They'll probably just talk about the creepy guy in the bar for a week," Emma agreed, laughing.

"Seriously, are you sure you don't want to have some?"

"I am positive," Emma assured him. "I just… I waited too long to eat and I don't feel well enough to risk eating that level of deep fried junk food. And the inappropriate jokes may have ruined mozza sticks for me forever."

"You love it," Scott teased.

"Not as much as you seem to like licking ranch off of phallic objects."

"Mmm, delicious ranch covered phallic symbols."

"You had better finish that," Emma warned.

"That's too much cheese," Scott said, pushing the plate toward Emma. "Eat it."

"No," Emma deadpanned. "God, just eat your damn cheese sticks."

Scott scowled as he picked up the last one. "It's cold and solid," he complained, picking off the breading. "Look at this. Would you eat this?"

"No, I wouldn't." Emma agreed. "And I wasn't going to anyway, and now you're just making a mess and being a weirdo."

"This should get chopped up and put on crackers."

"There are only like three minutes available in which mozzarella sticks are edible," Emma replied, shaking her head as Scott listlessly dipped the congealed mozza stick in ranch and took an unhappy bite. "And it's while they're the most edible temperature. Before that, they're molten lava, and after you get that cold, soggy consistency that you're currently experiencing and... why are you actually finishing it?"

"Because you told me I had to," Scott replied with a grin, eating the last bite of the last, cold, congealed mozza stick. "There, done. Happy?"

"No. I'm mildly unnerved, actually." Emma replied. "Do you always do what people tell you to do?"

"Depends on the person, I guess," Scott said, shrugging. "Apparently you can tell me to do stuff."

Emma grinned wolfishly and stuck her tongue out. "That is a power I should not be allowed to have, or exploit."

"Ah, now you're definitely trying to seduce me," Scott deadpanned.

"Is it working?" Emma asked, still grinning.

"I dunno. You did threaten to puke if I put anything in your mouth."

"I threatened to puke over your mozza stick."

"What? Oh, come *on*. That's not a very nice nickname."

Emma cracked up, burying her face in her hands, shoulders shaking as she laughed herself nearly to tears. "Why would you say that?" she whined into her palms. "Why would you even make that connection? You've ruined mozza sticks."

"They were ruined long before I started making blow job jokes," Scott replied, reaching out to pat her shoulder. "Do you require more comforting pats?"

"No!" Emma grumbled, shoving his hand away. "Should I stab you under the table again?"

"Ooh, those knives look fun and sharp."

Emma reached across the table to take one of the cutlery roll-ups, pulling the knife out of its napkin blanket. "Oh, yes, they are sharp. Do you want to take that risk?"

"I like this outfit," Scott replied. "These pants are my favourite."

Emma leaned over enough to look at what he was wearing. His pants were grey dress slacks and she sighed in defeat.

"Yeah, okay, those are nice, and you're wearing too many shirts to make it worth my while."

Scott looked down at his chest. He was wearing a vest, a sweater, a tie and a collared shirt. Fancy, compared to how he normally dressed in the store. "It's cold out," he offered as explanation.

"So that many layers means I'd have to stab you harder and it would just be a mess."

"So you lack conviction, too?" Scott teased.

"Lord, no. I'm just not willing to put that much effort into stabbing you today," Emma replied. "I kinda like your company."

"You're definitely trying to seduce me, aren't you?" Scott teased.

"Inviting you out to dinner wasn't your first clue?" Emma asked as the waitress returned to take their dinner order.

"You guys ready to order?"

"Oh, shit," Emma said, picking up a menu," I haven't even looked."

"I'm going to be super childish," Scott said.

"Why?" Emma asked.

"I'd like the mac n' cheese, please," Scott answered, addressing the waitress.

"Oh," Emma laughed. "Uh, I'll just have the buffalo chicken burger."

"Great, I'll be back in a few minutes."

"Thanks," Scott said with a smile as he picked up his Coke and took a sip.

They fell into companionable, easy silence for a long moment as they both sipped their drinks. Emma looked over at Scott who was slouching in his place. He looked tired, like something was wrong and was practically melting in his seat.

"Scott?" Emma asked, reaching a hand out to touch his where it rested against the table. "Are you okay?"

"Emmaaaaaaa?" Scott whined, looking over at her from here he'd slouched back. "I have a confession to make."

"Okay…" Emma replied slowly.

"I… I might be lactose intolerant."

Emma blinked in confusion and stared at him. A slow smile crept across her face and she started to laugh again, shoulders shaking uncontrollably. She patted Scott's hand before wiping away the tears welling up in her eyes. "Oh my God, that's it? What the hell?" she managed between peals of laughter. "You ate all the mozza sticks and then ordered mac n' cheese?"

"Well… yeah." Scott said. "I mean, I went for the tests once and it was inconclusive."

"Inconclusive?"

"Yeah, I figure it's like Schrodinger's lactose intolerance."

His answer cracked Emma up again and she dissolved into a laughing fit, burying her face in her hands and unable to talk for a solid minute. "Why then?"

"Why not."

Emma wiped away tears as she managed to compose herself. "Why didn't you tell me that when we fed you all that pizza?" she asked. "Now I feel bad."

Scott shrugged. "Not a big deal, and I like pizza."

"You're definitely an idiot."

"I just suck at being an adult."

Emma didn't argue that fact as their meals arrived. She stared mournfully at her plate. It didn't look appetizing in the least. She knew it was good though, she'd been coming to the pub for so long, there was nothing on the menu she didn't enjoy, it was just too late and she'd waited too long. Scott was in the same boat. He picked listlessly at his macaroni; taking a few bites and picking up the garlic toast it came with.

"You look wrecked," Scott said after a moment.

Emma picked up a fry and shrugged. "Too tired to eat and I waited too long."

"We're super good at adulting."

"You're the idiot who ate the whole order of mozza sticks and ordered mac n' cheese," Emma pointed out with a smirk. "But yeah, I'm pretty wrecked and no good at adulting today."

"I can't say that I approve of the fact that you didn't eat, but you wanna get out of here?" Scott asked. "I'm done."

"Yeah, let's go." Emma agreed.

Scott asked for the bill and for his dinner to go, Emma declined to take hers. The waitress returned with a single bill and Scott's mac n' cheese in a Styrofoam take out box.

"You want me to put it on my card?" Emma asked. "I don't have cash…"

"Neither do I," Scott said. "We're so good at this."

Emma laughed and shook her head. "We can just ask her to split the bill…"

"No, I got it," Scott replied adamantly. "But what about a tip. Do you feel you've been adequately serviced?"

"Not yet," Emma replied. "But you can fix that later."

Scott made a choking noise as Emma grinned and sipped the dregs of her Coke.

"My bank is on the corner on the way back to the train," she added. "I'll pay my half."

"You're not gonna let me pay, are you?"

"Nope."

"Ugh, fine," Scott agreed, reluctantly.

Emma smiled and stood, pulling a few dollars out of her wallet and leaving it on the table for a tip. She pulled her coat back on as Scott paid the bill.

"Where to now?" Emma asked when he came back.

Scott shrugged.

"You want to just head home?" Emma asked.

"Maybe," Scott agreed.

Emma smiled and led the way back out of the bar and into the cold night. "Bank first, though."

"Damn, thought you'd forgotten."

"I'm a woman, we never forget."

146

"And I'm never going to learn."

Emma laughed and linked her arm in his while they walked. She hadn't been kidding about the bank and she made him stop so she could get money from the bank machine. She held out a twenty-dollar bill and Scott just stared at her.

"What?" Emma asked

"I don't want it."

"Take the damn money," Emma snapped.

"You bought me pizza last time."

"Don't care," Emma insisted. "Do I have to shove this in your pocket or something?"

"Yes, like a stripper."

Emma laughed. "How much to I get for twenty bucks?"

"That's like maybe one layer."

"Including your coat?"

"No," Scott said thoughtfully. "I'll take that one off for free."

"But you're still wearing how many layers?"

"Do pants count as a separate layer?"

Emma shrugged and waved the money at Scott, which he took with a sigh.

"Fine, be that way," he grumbled.

"So…" Emma continued, looking at her almost empty wallet. "If you're wearing five layers, that's a hundred bucks to get you naked and dancing? I don't think I can afford that."

Scott laughed. "That's all right, it's too cold out here to strip anyway."

"You could always come back to my place," Emma muttered without thinking.

"I'm sure you staying with your mother would make that so much less awkward," Scott teased.

"Did I say that out loud?" Emma asked, pressing her lips together until they almost disappeared. "Oops."

Scott held his crooked arm out and Emma linked her arm back around his as he started walking back toward the train platform. He turned down a different street than Emma usually took to walk to the train and she had a moment of panic.

"Where are we going?"

"To the train," Scott promised. "Just… the more private way."

"Are you gonna murder me in an alley?"

"Yes, that's my plan and now you've ruined it."

"It would be so much easier to murder me in the park," Emma pointed out. "More likely to find a body over there anyway."

"Yeah, and there are more vagrants to blame it on…" Scott added, thoughtfully. "But that's the other direction."

"Well, we could go to the park for a bit, if you wanted?" Emma offered.

"As tempting as a brutal murder in the park is," Scott said slowly, "I think we're both far too tired for that."

Emma chuckled and pulled Scott a little closer as the wind picked up. "Okay, fine, no murdering me tonight. Maybe next time I buy some comics you don't agree on."

"Sounds like a plan," Scott agreed moving to cross the street.

"Wait," Emma said suddenly. "We're gonna get hit by a car."

"What car?" Scott asked motioning toward the empty street. Emma followed reluctantly, still with her arm linked around Scott's. They'd barely made it three steps across the street when a car came speeding around the corner.

"Holy *shit*!" Scott shouted, grabbing Emma's hand and pulling her into a run to cross the street before the car sped past them, honking as it did and disappearing into the neighbourhood across the train tracks.

"Told you so," Emma muttered, wrinkling her nose in distaste.

"Don't do that," Scott warned. "It's scary."

"I'm like Cassandra in Greek mythology," Emma joked. "I'm always right and no one listens to me."

Scott laughed as he walked her to the platform. She was going the opposite way to her mom's house, rather than the same way as Scott to get home. She looked up at the sign that dictated how long the next train would be. Thirteen minutes.

"That's not right," Emma muttered.

"You think so?" Scott asked.

"Yeah, the next one will be here in a minute, and then yours will show up right after."

"So I should go over there?" Scott asked, nodding toward the platform on the other side.

"Or you could hang out here with me and I'll catch the next one," Emma offered.

"But it's *cold* out."

"Yeah, but you're not gonna ride the train with me to where I need to go, and the next one after that will be in like five minutes, so you'll only be missing one train."

Scott opened his mouth to say something but Emma's train pulled up.

"Told you so."

"Now you're freaking me out," Scott said.

Emma grinned as her train pulled away and Scott's train pulled into the station. Scott stared, slack-jawed as her prediction came true.

"Stop that," Scott demanded.

Emma laughed. "Sorry, can't help it."

Scott shook his head. "At least the company is good."

"And you'll catch the next one," Emma said with a smile. "So? You wanna do this again sometime?"

"Yeah, I do." He stepped a little closer to Emma and she stared up at him. Everything froze for a moment and Emma was acutely aware of her heart hammering in her ears. Scott leaned forward and hesitated.

The train pulled up just in time.

Emma felt her heart drop as Scott wrapped her in a quick hug before shoving her toward the waiting train. "Get on your train and get home safely," he said quietly. "I'll see you for comics next week."

CHAPTER TWELVE

"He's so fun, and he's charming, and he's hilarious," Emma gushed, barely able to contain her excitement as she talked.

"You've been talking about this date of yours for like an hour," Stacey teased.

It had been an abnormally trying day in the kitchen and Emma's good mood from the night before had been the only thing to keep her from snapping at everyone else. Even Stacey couldn't help but smile the longer she had spent with Emma, even though she hadn't known what was going on until Emma had started gushing while they did the last load of dishes for the day.

"So it was a date?" Stacey asked.

"N... No." Emma frowned as she answered. "It was dinner, after work."

"That sounds like a date."

"It was maybe a date in the sense that we went out for dinner as friends," Emma said, her bubbly good mood waning as she thought it over. "I don't know that we're doing anything else but hanging out, but it was fun anyway."

"Sounds like a date."

"I asked him to dinner."

"So?" Stacey asked, giving Emma a look of disbelief. "What difference does that make?"

"It's weird, isn't it? Most guys get weird when the girl asks them out to do stuff. Like it emasculates them or something and makes everything weird for them."

"Did he?"

Emma shrugged.

"So what? You asked him out to dinner. I thought you guys were friends anyway."

"Yeah, we are."

"So then what's the big deal? He said yes. He followed through It's a date, and you're doing that thing where you overthink everything instead of going with the flow and letting things happen."

"You and your logic. And knowing me way too well for someone who barely sees me outside of work. You're ruining this," Emma teased.

"Oh please, " Stacey teased, flicking water in Emma's direction. "I couldn't ruin your mood over him if I tried. You're in too deep!"

"Sorry," Emma mumbled, unable to hide the grin crawling across her face.

"What are you apologizing for? This is the happiest I've seen you in forever, and believe me, it's infectious. It's hard to stay happy here, so the fact that you've been gushing over this not-date of yours means that I've had a reason to be happy, too. You deserve this, you work the hardest out of anyone in this damn kitchen, and you haven't murdered any of the other staff, even though you'd have been well within your rights to. Take the date and run with it."

"Still not a date," Emma muttered.

"And?"

"And nothing."

"Oh bullshit," Tracey hissed, dropping her voice so the kitchen manager didn't hear. "Admit that you wanted it to be a date."

"That's not even something I need to confess to," Emma replied, shaking her head. "You know it, I know it…"

"He doesn't?" Stacey asked.

"I don't know," Emma admitted.

"It was a date," Stacey confirmed with a knowing nod. "Trust me."

"Okay, *mom*," Emma replied, rolling her eyes.

Stacey laughed. "Look, you can either believe it was a date, or you can continue to doubt that it was anything more than a dinner, but which is going to make you happier and keep you from killing anyone in the last ten minutes of this day from hell?"

Emma laughed. "Okay, so let's say it was a date."

"Isn't admitting that so much easier than lying to yourself?"

"You do know that if this wasn't a date, I'm going to be very disappointed, right?"

Stacey made a hissing noise of disbelief and waved her hand, dismissing Emma's doubt. "Relax, kid. You had fun, you went for dinner, and you've been grinning like an idiot all day. Keep that. It's good for you."

Emma nodded slowly. "Yeah, you're right," she admitted.

"Wow, my kids never say that," Stacey replied, leaning heavily against the sink. "Hang on, I'm swooning a bit here. I feel dizzy and lightheaded. I don't know if I can keep working, you just said that I was right."

Emma laughed and flicked water in Stacey's direction. "You're so over-dramatic,"

"You're still young," Stacey replied, laughing as she tried to avoid the water. "When you have kids, and they don't listen to you, you'll get it."

"Ugh, that sucks," Emma replied. "Why don't your kids trust you?"

"The folly of youth is that you always think you're right and that experiences of anyone older than you is moot because of generational gaps. How can your parents' experiences be the same as yours when we didn't grow up with smartphones and the Internet?"

Emma stared at Stacey. "Where did that come from?"

155

"I'm not bitter about my kids refusing to listen to me, no sir," Stacey replied with a smirk.

Emma laughed. "All right," she replied, shaking her head. "You're just as insane as I am, I can dig that."

"You don't get as old as I am without picking up a little insanity."

"Duly noted."

Stacey laughed. "So, you had a good date."

"I had a very good date."

"See, told you it would be fine."

Emma glanced up at the clock on the wall. "Our shift is so over," she said, nodding toward the clock.

Stacey looked up and let out a little cheer under her breath. "I am so ready to get the hell out of here. Everyone else can clean up their damn mess."

"Amen," Emma agreed with a laugh. "Come on, we don't get overtime for this."

Stacey led the way out of the kitchen and to the locker rooms. Emma pulled her phone out of her pocket and touched the screen to check her texts. It had been buzzing in her pocket for hours. Emma made a little noise of gleeful shock and stopped on the stairs, leaning against the railing as she read the messages.

Stacey stopped when she noticed Emma's footsteps had stopped following her.

She turned around and eyed Emma. "You know you're not going to get paid overtime for playing on your phone, right?" She teased.

"I am perfectly aware of that," Emma replied. "And as much as I really don't want to be here any longer than is absolutely necessary right now, I can forgive this place for a few more minutes."

"Did you get good news or something?"

"Sure did," Emma replied with a grin.

"Oh, The Boy texted you."

"Yes he did."

"And?"

"It just says thank you for asking him out to dinner, it was fun, and he wants to know when I'll be back to visit."

"See?" Stacey said, triumphant and smiling like a Cheshire Cat. "Told you it was a date."

CHAPTER THIRTEEN

Emma almost didn't make it to the store the next week. Work had changed her rotation and she'd been working extra shifts to cover someone's vacation. It was Friday by the time she was able to make it back to the shop to pick up her comics and say hello to Scott. She'd been so busy she hadn't even had the time to send him a text and she felt terrible about it, but he honestly hadn't sent her any messages either, so she assumed he was either really mad and was being vindictive, or he'd been as equally as busy as she'd been that week. The latter seemed more probable and Emma hadn't really given it much of a thought.

Scott was standing behind the till when Emma walked in, working on something on the computer that acted as the register. He barely looked up as she walked in.

"I didn't think you were coming in this week," Scott said.

"And hello yourself," Emma replied airily. "I had considered coming in on Sunday, but decided that you'd be better off if I came in to say hi."

"That's cold," Scott teased. "You just disappear for a week after we had such a nice time the other night, and then you just expect me to be waiting here for you whenever you feel like you can bless me with your presence?"

"Yeah, that's basically how working retail in a store that I frequent works," Emma agreed with a nod.

Scott placed a dramatic fist over his heart. "You wound me."

"It's a just a flesh wound," Emma said. "I'm sure you'll get over it."

"Had a bad week?" Scott asked. "You're much more sarcastic than usual."

"I haven't been here all week," Emma agreed, nodding. "Bad is putting it lightly."

"Anyone die at work?"

"No."

"Did you *kill* anyone at work?"

"It was close," Emma admitted. "To be honest it was close on both counts, but the first part wasn't my fault. I was ready to commit murder and feed the bodies into the industrial garbage disposal."

"You sure you wouldn't have just…" Scott stopped mid-sentence as he caught the disapproving look Emma was giving him. He cleared his throat and grinned sheepishly. "Sorry you had such a shitty week."

Emma smirked and shook her head. "Thanks for the sympathies. You have no idea."

"I don't envy you, at least no one will die if something gets screwed up here."

"No, but I think walking in here poses a higher risk of murder than is generally considered normal for a retail setting."

"You say that like it's a bad thing," Scott teased. "And I haven't murdered anyone yet."

"Yeah, but I've seen you talk on the phone. Your eyes go completely dead and you do the PTSD thousand-yard stare better than anyone in the movies."

Scott laughed. "Yeah, I hate using the phone."

"I can tell," Emma said with a shrug. "Why do you think I don't call you?"

"Yeah, but if you called it would be way more fun."

"I'd ask you the most annoying questions, just to infuriate you, and you know it."

"Good point. Don't call me."

Emma laughed. "Then I guess I'll just have to keep coming in here to annoy you in person."

Scott shrugged. "That's not entirely a *bad* thing, you know. It'll be much easier to garrotte you in person than if you just called the store."

Emma arched an eyebrow as a wicked little smirk tugged at the corner of her lips. "And that's not your usual Tuesday night?"

"Getting garrotted?" Scott asked.

Emma shrugged. "I dunno, you might be into the weird stuff. Handcuffs and whips, I don't judge."

Scott made a face that was indecipherable to Emma and let the comment drop, which made Emma laugh and shake her head.

"Okay, I'll take that as a no, then."

"Well, I mean, Tuesday is such a weird night for that stuff," Scott said emotionlessly. "And Wednesdays are always so *busy* for me, it's just not feasible, really. I'd much rather be in bed at a reasonable time, and not be garrotted." He squinted, his face wrinkling as he pressed his lips together, rethinking his comment. "And garrotting isn't exactly something you necessarily *recover* from."

"Took you a minute to get to that conclusion, didn't it?" Emma asked.

"This is definitely not a normal conversation I'd expect to have on a Friday afternoon, in public, but it's far from the weirdest conversation I've ever had."

"I guess I'm not trying hard enough."

"You're going to have to try a *lot* harder to weird me out."

"I'm up for the challenge, then," Emma said with an easy shrug. "You're not the toughest nut to crack."

"What's that supposed to mean?"

"It means," Emma said, grinning widely and taking a step back, moving to head to the back shelves to find new releases, "that we should hang out on a Tuesday and I'll show you how hard you are to crack."

"Are you *trying* to seduce me?" Scott asked, imitating their jokes from their last dinner date.

"I'm trying," Emma agreed. "Doesn't seem to be working yet, though."

Scott glared at her as she walked away with a laugh. He didn't follow her, didn't leave his post at the register while she spent an extra long time browsing, and ignoring the trade issues of Daredevil on the regular shelf.

"So you're just a tease, then?" Scott asked as Emma returned to the counter holding a few books. "Here's your pull list, by the way."

Emma looked up at him with a wide-eyed look of innocence. "I have no idea what you're talking about," she said. "I would never tease you."

"I'm sure that's true," Scott replied with a shake of his head. "You're insane," he added for good measure.

"Ten percent psycho," Emma agreed. "But that never seemed to bother you before now. Admit it, you missed me this week."

"I don't know that I missed you, exactly," Scott replied. "But I'm not complaining that you're here today."

"Okay," Emma said flatly. "That's hurtful. We're even."

Scott laughed, "I'm so glad."

"Your sarcasm is showing," Emma pointed out. "I don't think that's entirely appropriate for a family-friendly store."

"There's a lot of inappropriate stuff going on in this store," Scott reminded her. "It's not entirely family-friendly."

"Well…" Emma started, and then stopped herself, shaking her head. "No, that answer is wholly inappropriate to make while standing here and bugging you at work."

"Now, I *have* to know."

Emma shook her head. "No, that's definitely something better left unsaid." She smiled. "But I was thinking, do you want to go hang out again? I mean, somewhere that isn't in the store so that we can be wholly inappropriate without worrying about getting in trouble?"

"As long as it's not another terrible movie night, yeah, I think that would be good."

"So, you don't want to come to my place and watch terrible movies with me?" Emma asked.

"Are we intentionally picking movies that are known to be bad?"

"Yeah, isn't that something you do?"

"It is," Scott agreed. "Those are the best kind of nights. So much sarcasm."

"Awesome, so next week?"

163

Scott hesitated, making a face as he thought about what his plans for the next week were. "Sure."

"Wednesday work okay for you?"

"After work."

"Yeah, I'll come get you," Emma said. "Since you don't know where I live. I'll cook."

"You can cook?"

Emma fixed Scott with an acid glare. "You want to run that one by me again?"

Scott laughed and held his hands up in a gesture of no contest. "I mean, I would love to join you," he corrected himself. "Next Wednesday, after work, heading to your place. Sounds like a plan."

"Awesome," Emma agreed, grinning and shaking her head, glad that her threatening glare hadn't been misinterpreted. "I'll see you next Wednesday."

CHAPTER FOURTEEN

Emma poked her head into the store. It was almost closing time and there was nothing new that she was reading out, and nothing on her pull list. She hadn't had a chance to get to the shop earlier; she'd gone grocery shopping and cleaned her house before getting ready to meet Scott. She'd managed to convince Mark to get out of the house so that she could have free run of the place without worrying about disrupting his usual schedule.

"Hey," she said with a small wave to Scott.

"Hey," he replied. "I'll be out as quick as I can."

"I'll just wait outside," Emma offered.

"You sure?"

"It's not snowing, I think I'll survive."

Scott laughed. "Okay, I'll hurry."

Emma smiled and stepped back outside. She leaned against the retaining wall by the door, standing on the sidewalk while she waited for Scott to close the tills. He didn't take long and Emma flashed him a bright smile when he joined her.

"Where to?" he asked.

"My place," Emma said, nodding toward the train platform a block away.

"We have to take the *train*?" Scott whined. "God, I don't think I can handle this."

"You bike everywhere," Emma reminded him. "It's not going to take that long."

"Yeah, but that's different," Scott whined. "There's no *people*."

"Shut up and get on the goddamn train."

Scott laughed and they walked to the platform. They didn't have to wait long for the train, and it was fairly empty. The bulk of the evening rush hour traffic had passed and they grabbed a seat.

"We're only going over like one stop," Emma said. "And then we have to catch a bus."

"Okay, no," Scott said. "I have to go. This is not happening. I refuse to take a bus, you didn't tell me that was part of the deal."

Emma laughed and tugged his coat, forcing back into the seat. "Shut up."

Scott let himself get pulled back down. "Okay, fine, but only because you promised me dinner tonight and I really don't want to cook.

"Oh, is that all I am to you?" Emma asked as the train pulled into their stop and she followed Scott off the train. "I'm a meal ticket?"

"Yeah, sure, why not?"

Emma shook her head. "You say the most romantic things."

"I'm good at that," Scott agreed. "Which stop are we going to?"

"The one across the street there," Emma pointed.

"It doesn't even have a *shelter*." Scott whined. "God, your life is so tragic."

Emma stared blankly at him and he laughed.

"You're going to murder me, aren't you?" Scott asked.

"Yeah. I live in a remote enough neighbourhood no one would call the cops if they heard you screaming like a girl as I murdered you."

"That's a terrifying concept."

"Welcome to living just off of downtown," Emma muttered as the bus pulled up. "It's never a dull moment."

"I don't believe you," Scott replied. "You're taking me to the outskirts of town, we're leaving the generally populated area of the city. You're going to murder me and bury me where no one will find me."

"Yeah, because taking public transportation to a murder is the smartest thing to do."

"I don't know how the mind of a serial killer works," Scott snapped with a grin. "I'm a cannibal, remember?"

"Remind me to never accept an invitation to your house for dinner," Emma muttered as the bus doors opened to let them on.

The bus was empty and Scott picked a seat in the middle of the bus and flopped down, patting the seat next to him in invitation for Emma to join him, which she did. They rode in silence for a few minutes, until the next stop when the bus nearly filled.

"Oh my God," Scott whined.

"They all get off in like three stops," Emma said, ignoring him.

"But now there's all these witnesses," Scott said. "I can't make rude jokes and threaten to murder half the city because of how much I hate taking public transportation."

Emma gave him an unamused, sideways glance. "Did you have that bad of a day at work?"

"No, it was a pretty good day, actually," Scott replied, his mood instantly shifting. "It was slow for a new comic book day, which is weird in general."

"Yeah but nothing came out this week," Emma pointed out, looking past him so she could see where they were.

"Plenty of stuff came out this week, you just don't read anything good." He frowned as he realized that Emma was staring out the window. "What's wrong with you?"

"I actually have no idea how to get to my house on the bus," Emma said slowly.

Scott's face paled and his eyes went wide, a look of momentary panic crossing his face.

"Just kidding," Emma said, reaching over to pull the stop cord. "Next stop is ours."

"Don't ever do that again," Scott grumbled.

"Why not?" Emma asked. "To be honest, I miss my stop at least once a day. Well, maybe one out of five times and I've already been out like three times today."

"You're evil, you know that, right?"

"Yep. I'm fully aware of it," Emma replied, leading the way off the bus and up to her house. "It's all part of the master plan."

"What master plan?"

"I hate to have to break it to you, but I'm not a human. I'm a lizard person and it's been my mission to figure out human weaknesses so my people can exploit them and we can take over."

"Yeah, I don't believe that, either."

"No, it's true. Why do you think I'm wearing so many clothes all the time? I'm freezing, this place is killing me."

Scott fixed Emma with a look that suggested that she was full of crap.

"I'm being serious, look," Emma insisted, reaching over and placing her freezing cold hand against Scott's face.

He flinched and pulled away. "Holy crap. How much farther to your house? That can't be healthy."

Emma nodded to the next house on the block as they walked. "That's home."

"Too dark to tell if it's cute, though."

"It's cute and little and kind of shitty, but it's home," Emma replied with a shrug, leading the way up the steps and unlocking the front door. "Come on in, make yourself at home."

Scott took his shoes and coat off and Emma held out her hand to take it. "Can't I just hang it on those hooks?"

Emma looked at the wall by the door as if she'd forgotten that the previous tenants had put two rows of coat hangers there. "I guess," she said with a crooked grin. "I was gonna hang it in the closet, and be a good hostess or whatever."

"This is fine," Scott said, hanging his coat on the hooks.

"Uh, I suppose I should give you the tour," Emma said. "Living room is right there." She pointed through the doorway in the hall. "Bathroom is there," she added, taking five steps. "That's my room, behind me through the closed door is Mark's messy as hell room and kitchen is there. Tour's done."

"That was easy," Scott said with a grin. "What are we doing?"

"I'm gonna cook," Emma replied, walking into the kitchen, with Scott following. "What's your preference?"

Scott shrugged. "I'm picky, but I'm not *that* picky."

Emma glared at him. "You suck. Make yourself comfy; I'll just make whatever, since you're going to be annoying. And I'm going to fill it with *cheese*."

Scott laughed, and sat down at the little table Emma had managed to fit into the small kitchen. It was cozy, with more cupboards than seemed necessary, and not enough counter space. It was nothing fancy, but it worked. Emma opened the fridge and made a humming noise as she tried to decide what to make. She'd gone grocery shopping before picking Scott up, so she wasn't hurting for choices, she just couldn't decide.

"Steak and rice and stir fry sound okay to you?" Emma asked, staring into the open fridge.

"Vegetables?" Scott asked. "Now I know you're trying to kill me."

"I'll take that as a yes," Emma replied, pulling out a package of steak and rummaging for vegetables in the crisper drawers. "How do you take your steak, by the way?"

"Uh…" Scott hesitated.

"That response means you're going to either say well done to the point of it being charcoal, or so rare that it's still mooing."

"The second one."

"Got it," Emma replied with a nod. She set about preparing the meal with a grin on her face.

"So do you cook for Mark?"

"Sometimes, when I'm home," Emma agreed. "He doesn't cook worth shit."

"That sucks."

"I'm assuming you cook?" Emma asked. "Since you've got such a weird diet."

"I'm a damn good cook," Scott confirmed. "But you'll never know that."

"Nope. Don't trust cannibals."

Scott laughed. "Can't say I blame you for that."

"It's all good," Emma drawled as she chopped vegetables. "I like cooking. It's therapeutic, stress relief."

"That's why you cook for a living?"

"I cook for a living because it was available, and if I had to do retail again I would probably actually kill someone," Emma replied. "But can we talk about anything other than work?"

"Yeah, let's do that," Scott agreed. "Like what?"

"Like… I have no clue," Emma admitted. "I don't actually do anything. I read books, and I buy comics that just go on the shelf and I never actually read them, I play video games sometimes, and I cook."

"You play video games?" Scott asked. "You don't really seem like the type."

"I know," Emma agreed. "I look like a girl."

"That's not what I meant, and you know it."

Emma laughed. "Sorry. What about you?"

"What about me?"

"I'm sure you do more than be a geek in the comic shop and bike everywhere."

"I do."

"So tell me," Emma said.

Scott took the invitation and started talking while Emma cooked, more than willing to tell her stories about all of his adventures. He was the kind of nerd who went outside and did things after he was done reading his comics.

"Why camping?" Emma asked as they sat down to eat.

"Why not?" Scott replied, cutting into his steak and poking it with his finger. "Holy shit, you did the blue rare properly."

"Yeah, don't people usually do it right?" Emma asked.

"Not really," Scott replied with a shrug. "Not home cooks, anyway."

"You get invited out to dinner a lot?"

Scott shrugged. "I get invited out a lot, and I usually say yes to invitations, but man, I'd love to just never go anywhere. Spend a week in a sensory deprivation tank."

"That would be a fun vacation, sure," Emma replied thoughtfully. "But I don't think I'd want to be alone in my head in the silence like that for that long. That's how super villains are made."

"You think I'm not already a super villain?"

"You're not super," Emma teased.

"Rude. I think I need to leave," Scott said with a grin.

Emma laughed and stood. "You want more?"

Scott shook his head. "No, I'm good."

Emma reached across the table and took his plate. She filled the sink with water and put all the dishes in, before putting the food away.

"Do you want help?"

"No, thanks for offering though. I'm just leaving them for now," Emma replied. "I'll wash them later."

"Are you sure?"

"Positive." She nodded. "Go pick a movie."

They settled on the couch in the living room and Emma handed Scott the controller for the game console that acted as a streaming device. "I have no idea how this thing works," she admitted. "It's Mark's, not mine."

Scott laughed and scrolled through the Netflix options. "Everything looks awful."

"Probably because it all is," Emma said, tucking her legs under her and leaning against the arm of the couch. They weren't sitting very close together, and Emma debating on moving over.

"Have you seen this one?" Scott asked, picking a comic book adaptation from a franchise popular in the 90's that some marketing executive decided needed a reboot for the current age.

"No," Emma said. "I have been avoiding this one on purpose."

"Is it that bad?" Scott asked.

"I don't know, I haven't seen it," Emma reiterated. "And I don't want to."

"Okay, we're totally watching this one."

"I hate you so much," Emma complained.

Scott grinned and started the movie, tucking the video game controller on the end table by his side of the couch. "You adore me," he replied.

Emma groaned and moved a little closer to Scott. "This better be…" she stopped mid-sentence as the opening sequence started to play. They looked at each other in abject horror at the poor job the movie had done translating the property to film.

"This is really bad," Scott said.

"I quit," Emma replied.

"We're like three minutes in."

"And I quit. It hurts my brain. This is so *bad*."

Scott grabbed Emma's knee. "You can't leave. You have to suffer. You made me watch the vampire-ghost movie."

"That Jane Austen Victorian ghost movie?" Emma asked.

"Edwardian," Scott corrected before he could stop himself.

Emma laughed. "Yeah, but, we paid for that one. You could stop this madness right now."

"Nope. We're watching it."

"You're the evil one in this relationship," Emma whined.

Scott laughed and was going to make another comment when a loud thumping noise interrupted him. "What the hell is that?"

Emma scowled.

Stomp! Stomp! Stomp!

"Mark is home," she grumbled, getting up as the door unlocked. "Hey Mark."

Mark smiled. "Hey."

"What are you doing here?" Emma asked through gritted teeth.

"My thing ended early, I came home."

Scott appeared from around the corner. "Hey."

"Oh, hi," Mark said.

"We're watching a movie," Emma explained glaring at Mark.

"Cool," Mark said, walking into the living room and sitting on the couch.

Scott took his seat back, too, striking up a conversation with Mark as they poked fun at the terrible movie. Emma sighed to herself, repressing the urge to punch Mark. She leaned on the back of the sofa, next to Scott's head. He leaned back, tilting his head so he could look at her.

"I'm going to do the dishes."

"But you're missing this excellent piece of cinema magic," Scott warned.

Emma shrugged. "I can miss five minutes and not miss anything. It's so bad, I need a minute anyway. Don't worry, I'll be right back." She didn't wait for Scott to argue. She knew the dishes would take longer than five minutes, but it was either do the dishes or fight Mark in front of Scott, and she figured the second choice wouldn't be the smartest way to end the evening. She had barely started when Scott appeared in the kitchen doorway.

"Are you sure you don't want help?"

Emma smiled. "I'm positive, I got this."

"Do you want company?"

Emma felt her heart melt a little at the offer, her anger with Mark slipping away. She shook her head. "I'm not gonna be long, I promise. Go watch the movie, I'll join you once this is finished."

Scott lingered a moment longer, like he was debating on arguing more, or staying with her while she did the dishes, but he nodded and left. Emma sighed to herself and washed the dishes as fast as she could, silently lamenting the fact that she didn't have a dishwasher. When she returned to the living room, the movie hadn't gotten any better and the boys were still making sarcastic comments back and forth about it. Emma leaned on the back of the sofa between the boys and looked at Mark.

"Didn't you have to go and do something with Dave?" Emma asked.

"Oh, shit, yeah, I forgot," Mark replied. "I'm an idiot. I'll text him and make sure that it's still cool if I go over there."

"Oh good," Emma mumbled as she took her spot back and joined Mark in watching the terrible movie they started.

It took a few minutes but Mark's phone buzzed. He grabbed it from the table and checked his messages. "Yeah, cool. Guess I'm still on for Dave. Gonna head over there now. See ya' later."

Emma didn't say anything as Mark got his boot and coat on and left the house with the same stomping as he'd arrived with. She huffed a sigh and got up from her spot, pulling her favourite blanket off the love seat and bringing it to the big couch where Scott was still sitting. She wrapped herself up in the blanket and curled up against the arm of the couch, away from Scott.

"You cold?" Scott asked.

"Lizard Person is not happy," Emma agreed with a chuckle. She looked over at Scott "You want some blankets?"

"Yes."

Emma grinned and rearranged the blanket so that she could drape it over Scott's lap. She scooted over, closing the distance between them on the couch and leaning against his shoulder, pulling the blanket up to her chin and tucking her legs up under her as the movie droned on.

"How much time is left in this awful thing?" Emma asked.

Scott picked up the controller and pressed a button. "Twenty minutes."

"Seriously?"

"I'm pretty much done with it," Scott admitted. "This is too bad even for me."

"*Finally*," Emma breathed in relief. "Turn it off. I don't even care."

Scott obliged. "Well now what?"

"Pick another something that's less terrible?" Emma suggested.

Scott started scrolling through what was available. Nothing looked appealing to either of them. "Want to just give up?" he asked.

"Yeah, okay," Emma agreed. "So what do you wanna do then?" She tilted her head so she was able to look up at Scott without sitting up.

"I dunno," Scott replied. "Do you have any suggestions?"

They stared at each other for a long moment, neither of them saying anything. Scott moved a little, leaning a little closer to Emma, but he stopped as they both heard a familiar and unwelcome stomping. Emma groaned under her breath and sat up, breaking the spell of the moment.

"Hey," Scott said sullenly as Mark announced his return. "Can I have your Wi-Fi password so I can figure out how to get home?"

CHAPTER FIFTEEN

As soon as Scott was gone, Emma stormed into the kitchen where Mark was making himself a cup of tea.

"You want some tea, Emma?" Mark asked, completely innocent and oblivious.

"You're the biggest asshole in the entire world," Emma snapped. "I don't want anything from you right now except maybe your head on a silver goddamn plate."

"Whoa, dude," Mark replied, "chill. What the hell?"

"Are you really that dense?" Emma asked.

"Yeah, apparently I am?"

"So you've got absolutely no clue why I'm as pissed as I am?"

Mark shrugged, his face completely innocent as he held his hands up.

"So you really can't read social cues, huh?"

"Yeah, apparently not because I have no idea why you're freaking out."

Emma growled a sigh and threw her hands up. "You're an idiot. You do realize that I had company, right?"

"Yeah, and I made plans to leave because of it."

"And then *you came home without texting me to warn me.*"

Mark blinked and stared at Emma who had folded her arms across her chest and was glaring.

"Oh…"

"And what makes it worse is that you did the same thing. Twice. In. One. Night." Her words were clipped, punctuated as she emphasized how really angry she was.

"I…"

"Like what the hell, Mark?" Emma asked, slouching against the wall and giving up. "You ass."

"I didn't think…"

"Yeah obviously not," Emma snapped.

"No I mean, I didn't think it was gonna be a big deal."

"*Dude.*"

"What?" Mark asked, completely innocent and oblivious to why Emma was so angry.

"Are you being serious right now?"

"Completely," Mark replied. "I don't get what you're so mad about."

"You know what?" Emma asked. "The next time you have someone over, especially the next time that you have a female someone over, I'm going to show up and walk in and not bother texting you to find out if you're doing anything or whatever. And then! I'm gonna sit my ass on the couch and watch TV with the person you're trying to spend time with."

"Okay?"

Emma glared at Mark, folding her arms over her chest and tapping her foot. "Seriously?"

Mark frowned and processed what Emma was saying. It took him a minute but he finally seemed to catch up to what Emma was saying. "Oh. Oh, shit. Oh… I mean."

"Yeah. Piss me off, Mark."

"Aw man, I'm sorry."

"You do realize it looks like you're super jealous right?"

"I'm not."

"Well it sure doesn't look that way," Emma snapped. "And the worst part is that you did it *twice*. I mean, sure the first time I could forgive. You're a complete moron, after all, but the second time? When you came back after I kicked your ass out once? Really?'

"I didn't even think…"

"No, you really didn't." Emma sighed and shook her head. "Thanks a lot."

"Emma?" Mark called as she stormed out of the room. "Emma, come back."

"No," she called. "I'm not talking to you. You're a selfish jerk and I really hate you right now. I'll consider forgiving you in the morning."

She slammed her bedroom door shut and flopped down onto her bed. She wasn't going to forgive Mark that easily. She just hoped that

Scott wouldn't be anywhere near as pissed off or embarrassed as she was.

CHAPTER SIXTEEN

"You look like you're ready to murder someone," Stacey said as she and Emma packed up their things after work. "You look like you've been ready to kill someone all day."

"Well, when these idiots can't do their job…" Emma complained before stopping herself. She sighed. She and Stacey hadn't had a chance to talk, work was a mess, things were falling apart around them, and they'd been the ones forced to clean up after everyone else and fix their problems. It didn't help that the dishwasher broke and maintenance wasn't able to fix it so they'd been forced into the dish pit for three hours, washing dishes by hand, rather than doing their actual jobs.

Stacey laughed. "Yeah, well, it's the nature of the job, welcome to kitchen work."

Emma shook her head. "The nature of kitchen work is for everyone else to be totally incompetent? And the fact that we can't swear on the floor? Corporate garbage. I don't want this."

"No one does. But you were mad when you got here. What's going on?"

Emma shook her head.

"Oh, did you break up with The Boy?"

185

"No," Emma sighed, flopping down into the plastic chair by the lockers and leaning forward. She cradled her head in her hands and breathed a heavy, tired sigh. "We're not a thing, anyway. Not dating."

"You sure do go out a lot for people who aren't dating."

"We've gone to dinner once, and out with a group of people twice. It's not really a dating thing."

"But something happened?"

"Yeah, kinda."

"And I'm assuming it wasn't good because you're not bouncing of the walls with giddy happiness. You're looking more like murder is the best option. Did he piss you off?"

"It wasn't him who pissed me off."

"Oooh, that sounds like a story I need to hear."

"Well, he came over for dinner last night," Emma explained, letting her hands drop and staring straight ahead. "I cooked, it was great. It was a nice meal, nothing fancy, but it was nice. Over dinner, we talked, he told me *everything*, and he didn't shut up for like two hours. It was fun. So then… We decided that we were going to watch movies."

"Sounds like a date to me," Stacey teased.

Emma felt her face flush and she folded herself up, flopping over until she was limp and resting her head almost on her knees. "It probably would have been, but we got like ten minutes into the movie and the roommate showed up."

Stacey made a noise that was somewhere between a groan of disappointment and a growl. "You're kidding?"

"I wish," Emma mumbled, sitting back up and resting her chin in her hands, elbows on her knees. "He didn't text or anything, either, just showed up. We were sitting on the couch, watching this terrible movie and laughing and all of a sudden, we hear stomping outside. He had gone out, he knew I had company coming over, and he just showed up. Apparently his whatever he went to do got cut short so he came home."

"That's brutal."

"That's not even the worst part," Emma sighed. "He sat down on the couch, decided he was gonna watch the movie with us until I kicked him out again."

"He did *what*?"

"He made his ass comfy on the couch."

"And the other one?"

Emma shrugged. "Scott? Didn't say anything, it's Mark's house, too, so he kinda just started joking around with him."

"Okay?" Stacey asked. "I have the feeling there's more to it than that?"

"I was so mad that I got up to wash dishes since I don't have a dishwasher. Scott comes to talk to me, I tell him I'll be right there, the movie was bad and I needed a minute, so I was just going to wash up the dishes from dinner and I'd be right back. Scott didn't argue. I go back into the room and I manage to convince Mark to get the hell out again, but he has to wait for a text. He leaves, eventually, excusing himself and getting the hell out of my hair. So, we're still sitting there, watching this movie. It hits a point where we're just done, it got too bad for us to bother finishing. At this point, I'm curled up on the couch, with a blanket and everything, so mad that I was just not into it anymore."

"Ooh, sweetie," Stacey cooed, placing a gentle hand on Emma's shoulder.

"Wait, this is the best part," Emma replied, sitting up properly so she could watch Stacey's reaction. "So we're looking for something else to watch, I'm leaning on his shoulder, I've thrown blankets at him and we're looking for another movie, but we're not finding anything interesting so we give up. We're sitting there, talking about nothing. It was really nice, I mean, don't get me wrong. And there was this moment. Just you know how everything stops?"

"Yeah…" Stacey said very slowly.

"Yeah, so we're sitting there and that kind of thing happened and I don't know if it was one of those movie moments where there's a whole big confession of love or what... And then... We just hear *stomping* coming up the front steps."

"You're shitting me."

Emma shook her head. "Mark showed up a second time without texting me after I'd already kicked him out once. So Scott asked for my Wi-Fi password so he could figure out how to get home from my place."

"Please tell me you broke your roommate's kneecaps?"

Emma laughed and shook her head. "Nope."

"That sucks."

"And the worst part is that I'm not going to be down there to grab comics for like two more weeks."

"So call him?"

"I don't want to," Emma said with a sigh. "I sent a text but he sucks at answering them."

"And you just let him get away with that?"

"Yeah, I'm not that good at texting, either," Emma pointed out. "So that's that. I have a cockblocking roommate and this huge embarrassment... that's not really an embarrassment, more like a disappointment."

"I'll say it was a disappointment, good Lord." Stacey patted Emma's shoulder. "I'm sure it'll be fine."

"Well, yeah, I guess, but Christmas is coming up and between the two of us taking all the extra shifts that we possibly can, I don't think that we're going to get a chance to go out again for a while."

"And?"

"And I hate this sort of not knowing feeling?"

"Well, I say you should kill the roommate and tell The Boy to move in with you."

Emma laughed. "Sure, that sounds like a great night. I'll just go to the shop, 'hey, you wanna come over for dinner? Yeah? Cool, bring a bag of quicklime, would you? I've just murdered Mark.' I'm sure he'd be totally into that."

"Hey, all guys know that girls are psycho."

"Yeah, but I think that puts me past the twelve percent psycho he said was his limit."

Stacey laughed. "Twelve percent?"

"We really do have the weirdest conversations, I haven't told you half of it."

"Apparently," Stacey mused with a smirk as she turned back to get her belongings out of her locker. "Well, look, it's not the end of the world, and if he hasn't sent you a text message saying that if you ever show up at the shop again, he'll kill you, then I say you've still got a chance."

"Thanks for the vote of confidence," Emma muttered, though she couldn't help but grin.

"You're welcome," Stacey said, earning herself a dry chuckle from Emma. "So when's the next time you get to go see him?"

"Like two weeks?" Emma said hesitantly. "Nothing's out this week."

"You could just go and *see* him, you know?"

"Shh, that's not a thing that can happen because I will end up buying comics that I'm not into and can't afford this close to Christmas."

"I thought you were done your shopping?"

"I am, which is why I can't afford comics," Emma joked.

Stacey laughed and pulled on her jacket. "Well then, there's no point in fretting over it, but knowing you, you'll do it anyway, so just try and relax and things will work out in the end, I promise. Besides, there's that old saying, 'absence makes the heart fonder' - which I normally think is a load of crap, but trust me on this. It'll all be fine whenever you get the chance to go back and say hello."

Emma sighed and nodded. She hoped that Stacey was right.

CHAPTER SEVENTEEN

Emma finally made it back to the comic shop. She'd been busy and MIA from keeping up with her comics, but at least there had been respite from her pull list as nothing had come out due to holiday hiatuses. She felt bad because she'd not had a chance to go and see Scott since their ruined dinner and a movie at her house, and she wondered just how mad Scott still was.

"Oh, hi," Scott said from his usual spot behind the till. "How are you?"

"I'm alive," Emma replied, setting her bag in its usual spot on the floor. "You?"

"Busy."

"It's always busy," Emma pointed out.

"Yeah, but holidays are coming up so there's been even more people expecting me to do my job and be pleasant and helpful and stuff."

"That must be such a pain," Emma teased with a grin. "People expecting you to do your job or whatever."

"Ugh," Scott replied, exaggerating the sigh. "Such an annoyance."

"You're so emo."

"I know," Scott joked, affecting a nasally tone and dropping his voice. "Everything is just so terrible and tragic and…"

"Are you wearing an ugly Christmas sweater?" Emma asked, interrupting Scott's ramble, and frowning as she stared at Scott's chest. "That's a nerdy as hell ugly sweater, oh my God."

"It's not ugly," Scott replied.

"No, it's really not," Emma agreed, "but was it supposed to be?"

"It's a super obscure sad robot reference in a Christmas sweater," Scott replied, looking down at the intricately knitted pattern. "I didn't know it was shiny when I ordered it, though." He added with a shrug.

"No, the shiny silver thread in the grey sweater makes it work," Emma agreed. "I like it, I'm kind of jealous."

"Because of the sheer disgusting levels of nerd this sweater radiates?" Scott asked. "Or because you don't have one? Or because it's just so damn sexy."

"Uh…" Emma replied, tapping her chin thoughtfully.

"Thanks," Scott interrupted. "Real nice of you."

Emma laughed. "You missed me, admit it." She shook her head. "It's a very nice sweater and I almost want to go figure out where to get one, but that would just be silly. I don't wear

Christmas sweaters. I have a friend who has a Christmas sweater that's got Krampus stealing kids on it. It's pretty rad, but I think I like yours better."

"I'm totally wearing this sweater every day for the next month."

"Ew."

"Doing laundry is for civilized people."

"God, Scott, that's so gross, but dammit, if I come back tomorrow and you're not wearing it…"

"You threatening me?"

"…I'll be very disappointed and won't stop whining about how disappointed I am," Emma finished, ignoring Scott's interruption.

Scott laughed. "So where the *hell* have you been? It's been what, two weeks? You've got a million comics waiting and we were getting mad."

"The royal we?" Emma asked, nonchalant because she knew he was screwing with her. "Or the we as in the owners of the store?"

Scott shrugged. "Royal, I guess."

"Got the ego out today, I see," Emma shot back. "Good to know what I'm in for then."

Scott opened his mouth to make some kind of witty comment but Emma sauntered down the aisles and disappeared from his sight as customers approached the till. Emma smirked to herself as she browsed the new releases.

There wasn't much out that she was super interested in, and yet another rehash of Batman didn't seem particularly appealing to her, considering that Christmas was coming up. She'd rather not delve into the gritty dark comics, it was a holiday for joy, damn it. Everything and everyone else was grim and stressed out, she didn't need her comics to echo the stress of the holidays. She picked up a single issue from the new releases shelf and shrugged, turning back toward the till.

"So are you going to get the three million comics in my file?" Emma drawled as she set her single choice down on the counter.

"I checked and you don't have any. How do you not have any?"

"I put like five things on my pull list," Emma replied with a shrug. "One doesn't start until February, one is on hiatus and everything else is basically pushed back because of Christmas."

"How do you only read five comics?"

"I also pick up a couple usual titles from the shelf but I'm not invested enough to put them on my pull list. Why?" Emma asked. "How many do you read?"

"Do you really want to know?"

"That many, huh?" Emma smirked and shook her head. "So you really do read *everything* everything, not just the elitist comic shop macho 'I read everything' crap."

"Yeah…" Scott hesitated.

"What?"

"My pull list is like thirty comics a month."

"Thirty?" Emma echoed.

"I cut it down from thirty-five."

"How the hell do you read that many?"

"How come you don't?"

Emma made a non-committal noise and ran a hand through her hair. "I'm pretty sure we've had this discussion, I do enjoy being able to pay my bills."

"Ah yeah, the whole 'I need electricity and food to live' argument that you made when you refused to buy Daredevil."

"Yep, that's basically it in a nutshell," Emma agreed.

"So overrated," Scott teased. "You know you want to buy the trades."

"Yes, and then I can build a house with all my comics and live there and have no need for food or electricity."

"Now you're getting it," Scott agreed with a nod.

"Oh, hey," Emma said suddenly. "I brought you something."

Scott eyed her suspiciously as she rounded the corner of the counter and crouched down by her backpack. She produced a large Tupperware container and held it over the gate, offering it to Scott.

"What's that?"

"Chocolate chip cookies."

Scott's eyes went wide and his face lit up with delight. "You brought me *cookies*?"

"I made them, yeah."

"When the hell did you have time to make cookies?" he asked, taking the proffered Tupperware and opening it. "Holy shit, why'd you bring me so many? You *are* trying to fatten me up so that when you chop me apart for food, I taste better!"

"You're the cannibal in this relationship, Scott, not me," Emma deadpanned.

"That's never been proven!" Scott shouted.

Emma laughed and shook her head. "Shh, relax, we're still in the store. Don't incriminate yourself more than you have to, God."

"Really, though, why so many?"

"It's only a dozen and a half," Emma replied. "And I made them yesterday."

"Why?"

"Because I said I would?" she said with a shrug. "I'm not really one to not go through with what I say I'm gonna do." A teasing, not-quite-malicious smirk crossed her lips. "I don't lack the conviction to go through with the shit I talk, unlike some people."

"Hey!" Scott argued, pointing an accusatory finger at Emma before taking a cookie and setting the container on the counter behind the till.

Emma tilted her head, cocking one hip as she folded her arms across her chest. "Hey what? I'm waiting."

Scott took a deep breath, opening his mouth and making a non-committal gesture with his free hand. "I actually don't have anything to really say about that," he replied, exhaling loudly in feigned defeat. "It's not exactly untrue, and I'm the one who said it in the first place. Do I always have to have a witty retort?"

"Yes," Emma said sagely, nodding slowly. "You can't just build something up and leave it hanging." She frowned to herself, wrinkling her nose. "That came out far more inappropriate than I intended it to."

"You said it, not me," Scott replied, taking a bite of his cookie before turning to help a customer waiting at the till. He turned back to Emma as the customer went to grab something from the shelves. "You're blushing."

"Shhhhhut up."

"Did you just embarrass yourself?"

"Shut up."

Scott chuckled dryly. "You're thinking inappropriate things, aren't you?"

Emma shook her head, trying desperately to keep a straight face, though it wasn't working. "Nope. I'm pure and chaste and innocent and I certainly never think or say lewd things to you, and especially not when you have a customer standing right there waiting for you to do your job and not eat chocolate chip cookies."

Scott turned and flashed the waiting customer a smile, moving Emma's single comic out of the way as he rang in the other customer. Emma took the chance to slip back into the aisles and compose herself while Scott was busy actually doing his job. By the time she managed to compose herself, there was no one else in the shop and she walked back up to the counter.

"Only the one, then for real?"

"Yes," Emma said, "stop trying to make me buy more stuff."

"So stop doing my job?"

"Yes, stop doing your job and let's just leave."

"I would love to, but the store isn't closed yet."

"I can wait."

"I have stuff to do after work," Scott replied flatly. "Sorry."

Emma shrugged. "Just thought I'd offer, make amends for the shitty roommate last time."

"Ha ha, he's got excellent timing," Scott teased. "It's all good."

Emma smiled thinly. "Okay, if you're sure."

"Whatever, I'm over it."

"I'm not."

"He *likes* you, you know."

"Ew."

Scott laughed as he rang Emma's order through. "So you'll be back in a bit?"

"God no," Emma replied. "I'm probably not coming back until after Christmas."

"Oh God," Scott whined, dragging out the syllables in his curse, and resting his head against his arms. "No, I don't want to deal with people doing holiday crap.

Emma reached out and patted his shoulder, before running her fingers through his hair. "Yeah, sorry, you'll just have to deal with everyone being terrible without me here to make it suck less."

"You're evil, you know that, right?" Scott mumbled into his arms.

Emma laughed and took her hand back as Scott sat back up, looking very tired and unimpressed. "I'm not evil, just misplaced in my goodness. Self-preservation over Christmas is way more important than you seem to think."

"I'm going to die."

"No you won't," Emma promised him. "If you do, I'd be super disappointed. You're more likely to snap and kill someone anyway."

"No. I'm pretty sure I'm going to die."

"Well then you won't get cookies," Emma pointed out.

"Good point," Scott sighed, eyeing the container of cookies on the counter. "Maybe I won't die, then."

"Atta boy," Emma teased. "I'll see you after Christmas."

CHAPTER EIGHTEEN

Stacey knew something was off before Emma even had the chance to say anything. They'd been on the same shift, but different areas of the kitchen and they hadn't had much time to talk on the line except to make sure things were prepared for the upcoming meal. Luckily, they were in able to take their lunch break together, and there was no one else in the break room while they ate. Emma had already settled herself at the end of one of the long tables, closest to the window where she could watch the door. She had unpacked her lunch and had a take-out bowl of salad and some Tupperware containers spread in front of her. She was playing idly with her phone and largely ignoring the food in front of her.

"Okay," Stacey said, pulling up a seat next to Emma and plunking herself down into the hard, plastic chair. "We're gonna share lunch and you're gonna spill your guts."

"I'm going to spill what guts?" Emma asked vaguely, her voice faraway and groggy, like she'd just been woken up from a nap.

"Your guts," Stacey replied, unpacking her lunch and handing Emma a mandarin orange.

Emma smiled and accepted the fruit, pushing her Tupperware containers filled with cheese and crackers toward Stacey. Stacey helped herself as she stared Emma down, waiting for her young friend to tell her the story of whatever it was that was bothering her.

"There's nothing to tell."

"There's obviously something to tell," Stacey replied easily, producing another orange from her lunch bag and peeling it for herself. "You've been walking around in a daze for a week. You haven't been smiling and bubbly like you usually are, and you're not talking about The Boy."

"Because I haven't seen him," Emma replied with a sigh, picking at the cheese and crackers she'd brought and passing over the salad in front of her. "It's been like two weeks since I went to the shop, and I already told you about the roommate."

"Yes you did. Did you ever kick his ass for that one?" Stacey asked, popping a piece of orange in her mouth. "Because if I was there I would so have broken a knee or something."

Emma chuckled and shook her head. "No. I mean, I yelled at him and explained that he was a giant jerk and I didn't forgive him for it, but, I dunno. I feel like it was stupid and that

203

we're kinda stuck in that weird friendzone space where neither of knows what the hell is going on."

"So go ask him?"

"Yeah, that doesn't really work," Emma said slowly, picking at her lunch. "It's not really a conversation I want to have in the store in case I'm the idiot who's reading too much into things, and I don't want to embarrass him, y'know?"

"I get it," Stacey agreed. "So why not make plans to go hang out again? Obviously you two get along."

"Yeah, we would, but we're both taking on all these extra hours, and it's right before Christmas, he's cranky and exhausted by the time he's done work, and my schedule isn't matching up worth a damn to even bother trying to make a dinner date or anything."

Stacey nodded and helped herself to Emma's crackers. "Okay, so just go visit him. You're moping around, what, no comics?"

"No," Emma agreed with a forlorn sigh. "The ones I'm reading are all on hiatus until after Christmas, so there's been no reason to bother going into the store, plus, it's Christmas. You know how insane all shopping places get when it's this close to a holiday."

"I do know, but you've got friends to shop for right? Get them comics for Christmas."

"Yeah, I'm already done all of my shopping and I am not going anywhere near a shopping mall or other retail store for the next two weeks if I can avoid it."

"What about groceries?"

Emma laughed. "Okay, so I'll go and get groceries and I'll be heading to my mom's this weekend for an early Christmas get-together but that's about it."

"So… why not go and say hello and take him a coffee?" Stacey suggested. "Stop in for five minutes, it won't kill you, and I'm sure he'd appreciate the gesture."

"Yeah, but…" Emma hesitated, staring into her bowl of untouched salad, as if there would be an answer there for her. No answer was forthcoming, and Emma frowned to herself. She didn't even know what she was arguing for anymore.

"You got very quiet," Stacey pointed out as she ate her sandwich. "You thinking? Or are you mad?"

"Not mad at you," Emma promised with a sigh. "I just don't know what to do anymore."

"You're still mad over the roommate thing, I can tell that much."

"It was so rude and stupid and I feel like it's put a wedge between me and Scott."

"Well, if it has, then you ought to go and fix it, don't you think?"

"Yes, probably, but we're not going to have time to hang out until maybe the New Year."

"So then go and pop in and say hi and take the entire staff cookies or something," Stacey said with an exasperated sigh. "You don't have to go just to see him, make it a trip with a purpose if it's too weird and say hi and make that the highlight of your trip!"

Emma opened her mouth and then closed it again, shaking her head and grinning. "I'm not friendly with everyone else, really," she admitted. "But you kind of gave me an idea so, thanks. I guess I will go and say hello."

"There's my girl," Stacey said with a chuckle. "All it took was some venting. And maybe you should slip some laxatives into your roommate's figgy pudding to get back at him for cockblocking you so hard."

Emma barked a sharp laugh and dissolved into a fit of giggles until tears streamed down her face.

"I'm so glad that I can amuse you," Stacey said, smiling widely. "Why are you laughing?"

Emma wiped tears from her face and shook her head. "Oh my God, I don't know why but you saying 'cockblocking' cracked me up. It tickled me, I'm sorry, it's awesome."

Stacey laughed. "Well, at least you're feeling better, right?"

"Much, yes. Thank you," Emma agreed. "So you have a plan?"

"I have sort of a plan. The beginnings of a plan."

"Does it involve laxatives in your roommate's coffee?"

Emma shook her head. "No, I'll let him live and I'll maybe, eventually, forgive him for that trespass." She waved her hand, dismissing the comment about Mark. "No, I think I will go and say hi to Scott, I'll drop in like you said. Won't stay long though."

"What are you planning?" Stacey asked, leaning in and dropping her voice to somewhere just above a whisper. "Are you gonna confess your love?"

"No," Emma said. "But it's Christmas, right? I'm going to spread some Christmas cheer."

CHAPTER NINETEEN

The door opened with a slow 'bing bong' as she slipped in out of the cold. It sounded tired, like a reflection of the feelings of everyone she'd spoken to on her way. It was the winter holidays, and everyone was in a scramble to make sure that Christmas was perfect. She'd never been happier to know that she was pretty much done shopping, having been smart enough to buy gifts for her family and closest friends back in November when her work bonus had come through, rather than waiting for December to roll around. She didn't envy anyone who had to work in a retail store during the holidays, and she hoped that it hadn't been too brutal of a day for the people inside the comic shop.

She stood in the entrance for a long moment, waiting for the feeling to come back into her rosy cheeks, and for the fog to finally lift from her glasses enough that she could wipe them on the hem of her skirt. As soon as Emma was relatively happy with her appearance, she poked her head into the main shop, peering around the corner.

It was fifteen minutes until closing and the staff were all standing behind the counter, chatting. Scott looked over as she stepped fully into view.

"Hey," he said, his voice flat. "What do you need?"

"Five minutes of your time?" Emma asked, hesitantly. He was obviously not in the greatest of moods, and Emma couldn't really blame him. It was the week before Christmas and while the store was surprisingly quiet given the calendar date, she was positive that it had been a busy day for everyone.

"I've got stuff to do," Scott replied, his voice still flat.

"I know, I just need… Five minutes after the store closes," Emma promised. "Maybe less than that."

"Why?"

"Because I need to borrow you for five minutes."

"Yeah, you said, but *why*?"

Emma's forehead furrowed in her frustration. "Good Lord, why do you have to be so cranky and stubborn?"

"Have you ever worked retail at Christmas?"

Emma chuckled. "Yeah, fair point. And you know I have. But I mean, just give me five minutes?"

Scott sighed. "Okay, five minutes, that's it. I have stuff to do."

"Okay," Emma agreed with a soft smile. "I promise it's nothing bad. I'll see you in about a half hour. Do you want a coffee?"

"No, I'm good."

Emma waved, pressing her lips together in a tight smile as she headed back out of the store and into the cold winter night. She walked with her hands shoved deep into her coat pockets as she hurried against the bitter wind to the coffee shop a block away from the comic store. It wasn't a far walk, but she sure as hell wasn't going to stand around in the cold for a half hour and wait for Scott to finish counting the till and closing the register. The coffee shop was warmer than it had been the last time she'd been there and she was thankful for that. The barista behind the counter smiled and she smiled back.

"Hey, you're back," the barista said.

"Yeah, I'm always back," Emma replied. "Is it cold out?"

"Not the worst, but cold enough that I don't want to stand around outside for a half hour."

"You're not here with your friend tonight?"

Emma felt the blush creep up into her face and was immediately thankful that the cold had already coloured her nose and cheeks a ruddy shade that masked the blush. "Na'ah, he's got work. I'm just killing time before I head home."

"That's always fun. You after tea, or coffee tonight?"

"I think I should have some tea," Emma admitted. "I've had way too much coffee for my own good."

"Did you work today?" the barista asked. "And do you want Earl Grey, or English Breakfast?"

"English Breakfast, please," Emma replied. "I didn't work today. It's my day off, thankfully."

"No comics?"

Emma laughed. "No, it's not Wednesday."

"You always have at least one on you," the barista pointed out as he handed her the steaming cup of tea. "Even when it's not Wednesday."

"The fact that you noticed almost weirds me out a little."

The Barista laughed. "Well, you're here all the time, and always when I'm on shift, and you're always reading comics in the back corner by the window. I don't think it's really hard to notice you when you're in on the same days every week."

"And you remember my order, which might be worse," Emma teased.

"I remember most of the regulars at this point," the barista said. "You're just the most pleasant to talk to."

Emma felt another bush creep up on her face and she pulled a five dollar bill out of her wallet and put it in the tip jar. "Flattery gets you so much," she joked.

"Ha ha," the barista replied. "Well, I appreciate that. It's been a quiet shift so far since all the shops close around here at six, and all the shoppers have gone home."

"You'll get the dinner rush," Emma said, taking the tea and blowing on it. "And the people heading home from the malls wanting a late night coffee before all the parties and stuff."

"I sure hope so," he replied. "Otherwise I'm going to be very bored and have a very ungenerous tip out."

"Are you all alone?"

"No, my partner is in the back doing stock. It's just boring and I don't feel like cleaning."

Emma laughed. "I feel that."

"What do you do?"

"Kitchen work, so I get the bored and not wanting to clean."

"Kindred spirits."

Emma laughed. "Something like that. Why don't you get some comics to read next time?"

"I might have to take that suggestion seriously."

"Always fun to pass the time, and way more interesting than the free newspapers."

"Have a good night, I'll see you next week?"

"Maybe not, I don't usually go out during the week before Christmas."

"Lucky you."

"I really am. It was just luck that I don't have to work and I've managed to do all my shopping except my groceries, which my roommate and I will pick up tonight or tomorrow."

"You have plans?"

"Not really," Emma said with a shrug. "Family Christmas always happens way earlier in the month, so that's done. I think I might just sleep in, make myself a frozen pizza for Christmas dinner, and watch superhero movies."

"Well that sounds great. I'll see you around, right?"

"Definitely. I can't abandon my usual hangout for long, comics happen every week after Christmas, anyway, right?"

"Do they?"

"They do," Emma agreed. "Have a great Christmas, if I don't see you," Emma said.

"Thanks, you too."

"I'm Emma, by the way."

"Benjamin."

"Have a wonderful Christmas, Benjamin."

"Thank you, Emma. You too. Goodnight."

Emma smiled and checked the time on her phone. She still had time to kill. She paid for her tea and set about doctoring it until it was creamy and honey-sweet, then she took her usual spot in the corner by the window and stared out into the night.

What the hell was she thinking? It was the week before Christmas, and she was waiting for Scott to get off work so she could what? Annoy him? She sighed and sipped at her tea. He was in a foul mood and she felt like a burden to ask for any time at all, but she wasn't going to back out. Five minutes wouldn't kill him; his plans could wait for that long. Besides, she wasn't asking him to go out of his way.

Emma's phone buzzed in her pocket and she felt her heart skip a beat.

She pulled up the text message. It was just her roommate asking where she was, and if she'd like to go grab dinner. She smiled to herself and replied that she was just heading to the comic shop and yes; she'd love to not cook, and wouldn't be opposed to take out.

The reply was almost instant and read: I'll come pick you up. I'll text you when I'm there.

Emma typed a slow reply. *Sounds good, I'll see you soon. Gotta do a thing first.*

She sipped her tea as the response read a single letter: K.

Emma sighed. At least that was her evening taken care of, she wouldn't keep Scott much longer than the five minutes she'd asked for, since she had dinner plans now. She drummed her fingers against the table top, waiting for time to move quicker. She was nervous, and she felt badly for asking for time when Scott obviously had things to do. She checked the time on her phone. It was 6:07. She sighed and got up from her spot, pulling her coat on and gulping down the last of her tea. She definitely wasn't going to keep him waiting any longer than she absolutely had to.

She threw out the paper cup on her way out the door and waved to Benjamin the barista as she left, inhaling sharply as the blast of cold winter air hit her and threatened to steal her breath. She walked quickly back to the comic shop, it was just a bit more than a block away and it didn't take her long to get there. She could see Scott still fiddling with something on the counter as she walked past the big windows, but he was wearing his coat so she knew she wouldn't have to wait long. It was probably a good thing, because she could already feel her hands getting icy cold as she waited. Leaning against the retaining wall by the parking lot she sighed and shoved her hands deeper into her pockets. The weather was turning colder and a fine snow had started to fall, filling the dark air with glittering ice crystals and making her feel like she was a snow globe. She was lost in thought and didn't notice when he stepped up beside her.

"You can't see anything with your hood up, can you?"

Emma laughed, doing a poor job of hiding the fact that he'd startled her. "No, I can't," she agreed, pulling her hood down and turning to look up at Scott. "Hey."

"Hey." He was slouching, his hands in his pockets and his face set in a blank mask that betrayed his crankiness and exhaustion.

"Please don't be cranky," she asked him, tilting her head slightly to look him over. He looked tired, and his body language was tense and defensive. He fidgeted and she knew that he had places to be and errands to run and she didn't want to keep him longer than she absolutely had to, but it was really nice to see him outside the context of the comic shop and she almost wanted to push her luck and try to convince him to come with her instead of doing whatever he needed to do that night.

"Ugh," he grunted in reply.

"No, seriously, don't be cranky."

"Retail is hell, and it's worse at Christmas," Scott grumbled, shaking his head and looking away with an exhausted sigh.

"I know, don't be cranky."

"People are complete animals, and I hate them."

"Don't be cranky."

"Why not?" Scott demanded, his voice taking on a sharp edge of annoyance in the face of Emma's quiet and gentle tone.

Emma smiled. "Don't be cranky," she repeated, pulling a small, wrapped package out of her pocket and holding it out to him. "Happy Christmas, don't be cranky."

There was a moment where everything stopped. Emma held her breath as she held out the gift, trying to keep her hands from trembling. Scott didn't react. He didn't move. He stared at the striped wrapping paper, then he looked at Emma. Everything stood still and Emma was extremely aware of her own heart beating in her ears. The frozen moment only lasted a heartbeat and the spell of worry was broken. Scott's shoulders relaxed and his whole body melted, all the tension and irritation in him running away like spring runoff. The coldness in his voice and face disappeared. His eyes lit up and his face split into the widest, most genuine smile Emma had ever seen, it was the kind of smile that brightened his face and made him glow. Emma let go of the breath she was holding and relaxed as he took the gift.

Scott stared at the gift in his hands for a moment. "I... You... It... What..." he stammered, unable to form a coherent sentence. He pressed his lips together and shook his head, the smile still glued to his face. "Thank you," he managed.

"You're welcome," Emma replied. "I think that's the first time since we've known each other that I've ever seen you actually speechless."

"You got me a gift?" he replied.

"Yeah," Emma said. "I thought that was obvious."

"Well, I mean, I wasn't expecting one, and I didn't get you anything."

"That's okay. I didn't tell you I had gotten you one."

"No, but, I've got to get you something now."

"You really don't."

"What do you want for Christmas?"

"Nothing."

"No, seriously."

"Seriously, nothing," Emma assured him. "I don't really go in for gifts all that much and I'm super impossible to shop for."

"Maybe I'll just get you..." he started.

"And if you get me a copy of..." Emma talked over him.

"...*Sam Wilson Captain America...*" they said at the same time.

Scott laughed.

"I'll kill you," Emma replied. "Although since it's *your* favourite thing, I suppose it would be fitting since I got you one of my favourites..."

"If you really don't want it..."

"I'd prefer it if you didn't get me comics."

"You're getting comics for Christmas," Scott said with a firm nod.

"Not from you," Emma teased. "You're not allowed to get me anything. I'm sure I will wake up to comics in my mailbox from the friends out of town who I sent all those autographed back issues to, which will be interesting, for sure. Besides, I think I've taken up more than five minutes of your time now, haven't I?"

Scott shuffled, shifting his weight from foot to foot. He frowned briefly. "I mean, it's not like you have to go this very second."

"Don't you have errands?"

"I do, and I'm on a tight schedule. And I'm probably already running late."

"So go," Emma said. "It's all good. I'm meeting the roommate for dinner anyway."

"Like a date?"

"Like I don't wanna cook and we're both exhausted so we're going to drink shitty coffee and eat food that is, generally speaking, bad for us."

"Sounds like a date."

Emma shuddered. "No, definitely not a date."

"You could come with me…"

"You're gonna take off running and I'm short, and definitely can't keep up, so really, go on, do your errands. Have a wonderful night, and a good Christmas."

"Thank you," Scott said with a nod.

They stood there for a long moment, staring at each other, silently as the fine sprinkling of snow fell across their shoulders, glittering in the light like fairy dust. Scott still held the gift Emma had given him in one hand and Emma held her hands together, desperately trying to keep them warm. Scott moved a little closer, shifting just slightly and leaning forward.

Emma's phone chirped in her pocket, a sound effect from a video game, and the spell of silent admiration was broken.

"That's the roommate," Emma mumbled.

"Always with such excellent timing," Scott replied.

Emma sighed and shook her head as she checked the text message. "Yeah, he's waiting for me."

Scott smiled, tight-lipped and slightly disappointed. "Well, better go meet him then."

"You're welcome to come for dinner," Emma offered weakly.

"I would, but I have this stuff to do."

Emma nodded. "I know." She held her arms out and Scott took the invitation. She leaned up on her tiptoes to give herself some height against him, and to avoid having her face smushed against his chest as he wrapped his arms around her in a hug. She found her cheek pressed into his neck and she felt momentarily bad for being as cold as she was against the bare skin under his collar.

"You're way warmer than I am," Emma muttered. "This is bullshit. Lizard-person is not happy."

Scott laughed. "You're not that cold."

Emma touched her fingers against his cheek and he pulled back with an unhappy noise, breaking the hug as Emma laughed and shoved her hands back into her coat pockets.

"Holy shit."

"Told you."

"Go home and warm up."

"Yeah, eventually," Emma agreed. "Dinner first."

"Have fun."

"Have a good Christmas. Don't murder anybody."

"No promises."

"I won't see you 'til next year."

A look of momentary confusion crossed Scott's face as he registered what Emma had just said. He huffed a sigh and shook his head. "That is a horrible joke and now I'm not talking to you for a week."

"That's fine, I won't be back 'til there's new comics anyway, and I sure as hell won't be in during the last couple shopping days before Christmas, so I think I can handle you ostracizing me for a week."

"Go home."

Emma smiled brightly. "All right," she agreed. "But I'm heading this way," she added, pointing toward the corner. "Roommate is somewhere over there."

Scott shook his head. "I'll walk at least that way with you."

"Sounds good," Emma agreed as they set off. Scott slowed his pace to match Emma's and didn't whine about it, which was a pleasant change of pace for Emma. She couldn't help being short, and while his generally good-natured banter over their height differences would have been welcomed, it was obvious that Scott wasn't entirely in the mood to hang out. Not that she could blame him.

"You're fidgeting," Emma pointed out as they walked away from the comic shop and down the brightly lit, but empty sidewalk. "You're nervous, and you're late, go. I won't be upset."

"You sure?"

"Roommate has a car," Emma pointed out. "And he's just at the grocery store in the parking lot."

"Okay. Thanks again. Have a good night."

"See you when I see you."

"Merry Christmas," Scott replied, waving as he took off, heading away from Emma and practically sprinting down the street.

Emma smiled to herself, a spring in her step despite the disappointment of Scott not joining her for dinner, as she headed across the grocery store parking lot to find her roommate's car.

223

CHAPTER TWENTY

The New Year rang in with very little ceremony for Emma. She'd played video games with her roommate until she got a headache and went to bed shortly after the clock rolled over to midnight. She wasn't as lucky as her roommate to get the time off after the holidays, and she still had to go to work like a functional adult, despite not feeling like one. Mark had very little sympathy for her and he bid her a fond farewell from the couch the next day where he was camped out in his pyjamas and playing video games. Emma ignored him and went to work.

And then she did it again the next day.

It wasn't Wednesday when she managed to find the time to get back to the comic shop. At least her pull box was only two issues, and the previous week had been nothing so she didn't feel too guilty about not having the time to actually get to the shop and get her comics. The holidays were good for delaying releases for a few weeks; it was enough time for her wallet to recover from the frenzy of holiday shopping.

The store was busier than she'd seen it in a while, especially for it not being a new comic book day and one of the departing customers held the door open for her on her way in.

Emma winced at the volume of people in the shop. It wasn't holiday busy by any stretch of the imagination, but it certainly wasn't as quiet as usual.

Scott was helping a customer at the till and he flashed her a quick smile as she edged her way around the till and to the back of the store to check what other new releases had come out that she hadn't put on her pull list. There were a lot of new releases and Emma couldn't help but cringe with every issue that she picked up. All of her favourites were staring her in the face and she muttered swears under her breath as she picked up yet another title to try out. She very quietly muttered 'fuck this' as she picked up one issue and decided against it. Her wallet was already crying as she mentally tallied up how much she was spending this close after Christmas. With a defeated sigh, she picked up the last issue she'd been debating on and shuffled her way to the till.

Scott flashed her a grin as she set down her stack of comics. "That's a lot of comics."

"Oh good you're not dead," Emma replied.

"Oh, I'm dead, don't worry, I'm just a ghost."

Emma laughed once and shook her head. "You're awfully solid for a ghost."

"And I can move stuff around."

"And considering where you're standing, you probably want all my money."

Scott frowned and bobbed his head back and forth in a non-committal way.

"I'm pretty sure," Emma pointed out, "that was the plot of that movie we saw that time."

"Don't remind me about that movie," Scott complained.

"So are you a ghost, then?"

"We're all ghosts, Emma. We're all just temporarily inhabiting these fleshy prisons until we die and are freed of our mortal bodies and can become the ghosts that we all know that we truly are on the inside."

"So you've been spending too much time on the internet this week," Emma replied.

"So much. I don't even want to talk to anyone ever again."

"Sorry, I'll just throw money at you and leave."

Scott laughed. "I love it when people throw money at me."

"You'd better dance for it, then," Emma replied with a smirk.

"Dancing no. I'd rather just take my clothes off."

"All five layers you're wearing? That could take a while and I'm not sure I have enough cash on me to get past the vest."

Scott looked down at his outfit and counted out his layers. "Three. I'm wearing a vest, a sweater and a collared shirt."

"And a tie, that's gotta count for at least one layer."

"You're talking yourself out a strip show, you realize this, right?" Scott pointed out.

"I am fully aware that I cannot afford your stripping in the store today," Emma agreed. "I spent far too much money at Christmas to pay for a show."

Scott laughed. "Your loss."

Emma shrugged and held up a hand in a gesture of no contest. "I will just have to deal with missing out on yet another one of your five-layered stripteases. Will you go get my pull list, please?"

"Is there anything even *on* your pull list this week?" Scott asked. "You only have like three things on there and you're getting all the crap off my shelves."

"I have five on my pull list, thank you," Emma replied matter-of-factly. "And yes, there's none from this week but there's two from last week, but I forget which ones."

"All right, if you say so," Scott said with a shrug before disappearing into the back room behind the till where the boxes of pull lists were kept. Emma waited, fidgeting with the corner of one of the books she was picking up. Scott returned momentarily, holding two single, slim issues from her file.

"Huh, you were right."

"I'm always right," Emma teased.

"No, *I'm* always right. You just got lucky."

"I'm a woman," Emma reminded him. "I'm *always* right."

"Touché."

"So you managed not to die over Christmas," Emma continued, changing the subject. "You murder anyone?"

"It was close."

"That bad, huh?"

"It wasn't even really *Christmas* that made people go insane. It was after."

"Seriously?"

"I… It's a long story, and I'm getting mad just thinking about it."

Emma grimaced. "I do not envy you these past few weeks."

"I just want a sensory deprivation chamber and a week off."

"I can't make either of those things happen," Emma said slowly. "But, you wanna go get coffee and vent?"

"I'm working."

"After, you idiot."

"Idiot?" Scott said, feigning hurt and clasping a hand to his chest. "That wounds me. I'm not an idiot."

"You sure?"

"I am a jackass and a hipster, not an idiot."

"All right, you hipster jackass." Emma corrected herself with a grin. "You wanna go get coffee after you're done working?"

"Sure."

"That wasn't difficult, was it?" Emma teased.

"Well since you're not inviting me to go hide in a sensory deprivation chamber, yeah, it's difficult to say yes."

Emma groaned and rolled her eyes. "I'm so sorry I don't have a sensory deprivation chamber where I can shove you and lock you away from the ghosts of Christmas retail."

"You should be," Scott teased. "How are you paying?"

CHAPTER TWENTY-ONE

Emma waited for Scott to close the till. It was cold outside and she didn't feel like sitting around outside the shop, but he promised he'd be quick, it hadn't been very busy and he swore it would only take ten minutes for him to count out the day's sales.

Emma scowled to herself as the wind bit through her woollen coat and she pulled her phone out of her pocket to glare at the time. It had been more than ten minutes and she would have to give Scott a stern talking to about that.

She knew she could walk over to the coffee shop, she knew he wasn't going to just leave her alone without explanation, but it seemed to Emma that it would be somehow mean to leave him and make him walk alone, even if it only was a block and a half. Besides, she didn't know what he would drink since he didn't drink coffee, and it would be rude to order something for herself and to be drinking a beverage of some kind if she didn't have something for him. She had manners, after all, even if it didn't seem like it sometimes. She tried to hunker down and pull her coat around her more, to little avail. The wind was cold enough to bite through the material and she cursed herself for not bringing warmer gloves.

Scott finally appeared in the door and Emma breathed a little sigh of relief as he stomped down the steps. "You didn't have to wait for me, I wouldn't ditch you, you know."

Emma smiled. "I know, but it seemed rude."

"You look frozen."

"Close."

"Come on, Lizard-person, let's get you coffee."

Emma laughed, she didn't think he'd have remembered her offhand comment about being a lizard person, but she appreciated it anyway. She didn't complain that Scott was walking faster than she was normally comfortable with keeping up with, the cold had made her want to get inside as quickly as possible and she didn't mind the fact that she was practically jogging to keep up with his long strides. The wind was bitter and she just wanted a cup of coffee to warm up.

"I'm so sorry you waited out here in the cold like that," Scott said as they stopped at the crosswalk. "I didn't know you were actually going to wait outside."

"It's okay," Emma said with a shrug. "It's my own damn fault that I didn't wear enough sweaters to keep me warm."

"How many sweaters does a lizard person need to stay warm?"

"About seven. Or a blanket."

"That seems like an unreasonable number of sweaters."

Emma glanced up at Scott. "You've met me. Seven seems like a perfectly logical number of sweaters to keep me warm. It's finding seven sweaters that will stack comfortably that's the problem."

Scott laughed and shook his head at the ridiculousness. "Does Mark know you're out here with me?"

"I'm an adult," Emma replied flatly. "I don't need to tell him my every single move."

"How are you getting home?"

"Dude, its six o'clock on a Wednesday. I mean, I know it's dark out, but nothing has shut down. I'll take the bus, it's not like I'm going to get murdered in an alley."

Scott laughed. "Sorry, it's just been a really long couple of weeks and I'm beyond tired and paranoia is kind of the defence mechanism I turn up when I get this tired."

"Well I appreciate you looking out for me," Emma said with a smile as they crossed the street. "I promise I'll be fine. I made it home after ten on that one dinner night, despite almost getting hit by a car because *someone* doesn't like to listen."

"Oh yeah," Scott replied. "I guess I forgot."

"You forget a lot of random things, don't you?"

"Only when it involves me being completely embarrassed."

"Are you actually embarrassed, or are you just being a smart ass?"

"I'm totally being a smart ass," Scott confirmed. "But if it's easier just to call Mark to get home, I'm not going to hold that against you."

"No harm in making sure I can get home safely. Worst case, I'll actually call Mark for a ride home, but I don't think there's any reason to. It's early and I don't live that far away, really." She shrugged as Scott held open the door for her. She sighed and took her glasses off before stepping into the warm coffee shop interior.

Scott gave her a confused look as he watched her take her glasses off. She held them up to show him the fog forming on the lenses and he laughed. "I've never seen anyone do that."

"Way better than sitting here and not being able to see a damn thing," Emma replied nonchalantly. She wiped the fog away with the hem of her skirt. She'd never been happier to be wearing thick leggings underneath the red dress she was wearing, even if she was mad that she'd only worn one sweater.

"Do you always wear skirts?" Scott asked as they moved into the cafe proper. "I don't think I've ever seen you dress like a normal person."

"You mean wear pants?" Emma asked.

"Or colours," Scott added.

Emma laughed. "Because my coat is grey?"

"And because you normally wear black, so the red skirt is a little weird."

"You notice what I wear?" Emma asked with a smirk. "Do you know what kind of coffee I drink, too?"

"No," Scott admitted. "But I've never seen you order a coffee before."

"Well, I'm ordering a tea tonight, so you'll just have to keep wondering," Emma teased. "And yes, I do wear pants sometimes, I have to wear a uniform to work, kitchen pants and stuff, so I prefer not to wear them when I'm not at work."

"Well, you look good," Scott offered.

Emma wrinkled her nose as she smiled. "Thanks," she replied. "What are you drinking? I'll buy."

"Uh." Scott stammered, staring up at the menu. "Hot chocolate."

"Aren't you lactose intolerant?" Emma asked.

"I'll be fine."

"It's your funeral," Emma teased as she stepped up to the counter.

Benjamin wasn't working and Emma felt her heart sink. He was always at the cafe on Wednesdays. She placed their order and made sure that the strange barista heard her say no whipped cream on top of the hot chocolate. She took her tea and added milk and honey while Scott waited for his drink. She smiled at Scott and he pointed to her favourite booth by the back window. The cafe was half full, but her usual spot was empty. She nodded and Scott thanked the barista as he took his drink and led the way to the back corner. He took his usual spot on the high bar style chair, leaving the booth seat open for Emma. She slipped into her comfy spot and tucked her bag and her coat next to her as she relaxed against the booth.

It took her a moment to catch the look that Scott was giving her and a flash of panic went through her. Was there something on her face? Did she spill something on her shirt? Was her makeup running?

"What's that look for?" Emma asked, feeling entirely self-conscious in that moment, and touching a hand to her face like she could undo whatever horror her face had inflicted by covering it up.

"You're wearing a Captain America hoodie." Scott replied. "You don't even *like* Captain America."

Emma blinked back her confusion and stared down at her chest. "Oh my God! You're right! How did this happen? Where did this come from? I don't even know who it's supposed to be, I just liked the star on my boobs. God, I am such a fake geek girl."

"Okay, that's sarcasm," Scott pointed out. "I get it, chill."

Emma grinned. "It was a gift from Mark."

"But…"

"I never said I didn't like Captain America, I just said I didn't feel like reading Sam Wilson because ugh, politics in my funny books."

"See?" Scott conceded around a sip of hot chocolate. "You have terrible taste in comics."

"You're such an ass," Emma replied, shaking her head.

"You can always stop hanging around if it's a problem," Scott teased. "I don't work on Sundays."

"I gotta have someone to keep me on my toes," Emma said with a shrug as she sipped her tea. "How was Christmas?"

"I honestly don't want to talk about it."

"You wanted to talk about it like ten minutes ago," Emma pointed out.

"Yeah, but ten minutes ago I was still at work and didn't have hot chocolate."

"Was it really that bad?"

"You have no idea," Scott said, shaking his head. "People are animals, it's horrifying."

"Well, yeah, that's kind of the first thing you told me when I gave you your gift."

"I don't get it, people are just so cranky and demanding over the holidays."

"Stress will do that."

"Yeah, but taking it out on me? And then getting mad when I tell them that we can't do exchanges the day after Christmas?"

"People get fussy over their gifts," Emma offered weakly. "Speaking of gifts. There was a gift receipt inside…"

"I kept it," Scott interrupted, almost offended at the suggestion.

"I wouldn't be offended if you didn't like it," Emma added with a shrug. "It's one of my favourites, I thought you might like it, but then I realized that I have no idea if you even read books that don't have pictures in them."

"Well, I do," Scott said. "I am a functioning human adult who is capable of reading books with no pictures in them. Pictures aren't everything. I just… I haven't read it yet because I got like a dozen books for Christmas."

"Oh, good, I wasn't that far off, then," Emma replied with a sigh of relief. "I kinda just give everyone books when I don't know them very well."

"Yeah? That's cool. Everyone got me books this year. It was weird."

"Would you have preferred socks?"

Scott laughed, loudly, drawing a few irritated looks from the other guests in the cafe, which he promptly ignored. "They'd have to be extremely awesome socks."

"Noted," Emma said, nodding. "Maybe for your birthday."

Scott opened his mouth to reply and then closed it again, changing his mind and sipping his drink instead. "What about you?" he asked. "You had Christmas, didn't you?"

"I sat around at home by myself and watched superhero movies, just like I said I was going to," Emma said. "I didn't go anywhere, I didn't have to cook. I slept in for the first time in months, and made myself a nice breakfast and then had frozen finger foods for dinner. No roommate, no family, just me and movies. "

"Sounds like heaven."

"You could have come over," Emma reminded him. "I offered."

"Yeah, well, you know how it is when you make plans."

"Plans can be changed," she teased. "It's all good, man. It wasn't as lonely as I thought it would be, just another day, and I was back at work the very next day anyway."

"You didn't get any time off?"

"I had Christmas Day off." Emma shrugged. "You had to work, too."

"Yeah, but… your job seems somehow less pleasant to work over Christmas."

Emma smiled sadly. "Yeah, it was hard. I feel bad for anyone who had to go there on Christmas Day. I couldn't have. I'd have been wrecked."

"Sorry."

Emma shrugged again and sipped her tea. "What about New Year's? Do you party?"

"Sometimes," Scott replied, weighing his answer. "I think my terrible friends are planning a lot of drinks."

Emma laughed and nodded. "That sounds like fun."

"You gonna pull the alone on New Year's thing, too?"

"Probably."

"That sounds less than fun."

"I have video games and books," Emma replied. "Plus, I'm pretty sure I work on New Year's Day, so it's not like I could go party anyway."

"That super sucks."

"Extra money is always nice."

"I cannot argue with that." Scott agreed, tipping his cup in a toast before gulping down the rest of his hot chocolate. They fell into momentary companionable silence and Emma noted that Scott was fidgeting with the paper cup in his hands.

"You want to go, don't you?" Emma asked.

"How can you always tell?"

"You get fidgety and antsy," she replied. "It shows in your body language."

"I do not."

"You get like that at the shop when we hang out for too long and you feel like you need to do something productive," Emma continued. "You get antsy when it takes too long for anything to happen or you're feeling uncomfortable."

"So you just watch me and then pick apart all my habits?" Scott asked, incredulous, but impressed. "Going full Sherlock on me?"

"Not intentionally," Emma replied, finishing her tea and grinning. "That's just the one that I've noticed the most. Sorry."

Scott shrugged. "I didn't even notice it about myself."

"It's 'cause it's your habit," Emma replied, standing up and picking up her coat. "Do you want to get out of here?"

"Yeah…"

Scott stood and pulled on his jacket and Emma did the same, before she picked up her bag and her empty paper cup. She followed him out of the cafe, and he held the door for her.

"I hate winter," Emma mumbled as she zipped up her jacket.

"Yeah, it's a pain."

"Too cold for Lizard Person," Emma grumbled.

Scott laughed. "You taking the train?"

"Yeah, I didn't call Mark." She looked up at Scott. "Why? You wanna ditch me?"

"No," Scott replied, huffing a sigh. "Unless you want me to?"

"I'd rather you didn't," Emma admitted. "We're going the same way anyway."

Emma linked her arm through Scott's as they walked to the train platform. They crossed the street and walked up the ramp to wait for their ride. Scott glanced up at the flashing sign above their heads. Two minutes for the next train.

"It's never accurate," Emma said.

"Don't start with that again," Scott warned. "How many trains did we miss last time?"

"Only one each," Emma replied with a giggle. "But I was staying with my mom so I was going the opposite way."

"And how many are we going to miss tonight?" Scott asked, stepping a little closer to Emma.

241

"I don't know yet… Are you suggesting we go somewhere else?" Emma asked, looking up at him. "I mean, it's early, I don't have to be anywhere."

"Haven't decided," Scott replied, closing the little distance between them until they were almost touching. "I just don't think I want to ditch you just yet."

"I'm not complaining about that." Emma assured him. "Did you have something in mind?"

"Did you?"

Emma shrugged and looked away, trying desperately to neither blush, nor make the sarcastic, slightly off-colour comment that sprang to mind when he'd asked. There was a damn good chance that he was at least a little bit psychic because he laughed quietly in the face of her lack of response.

"Whatever you're thinking, as long as it doesn't end in murder or cannibalism, I'm probably not going to argue."

"And if it does?"

Scott shrugged. "I'm willing to take that chance."

Emma chuckled and nodded up toward the sign. It still read two minutes for the next train. "Told you that it wasn't going to be accurate," she said. "We've been standing here for three minutes already."

Scott looked up at the sign. "Well, *fuck*."

"You say that like it's a bad thing."

"Well, it's cold out," Scott said. "And you're doing that thing where you're always right again."

"Sorry," Emma teased, glancing away.

"It's okay." Scott reached out and cupped her face in his hand, pulling her chin gently until she was looking at him. "I'm not really bothered by it. And I think I've decided what I want to do."

Emma arched an eyebrow as Scott leaned in, kissing her.

They only missed one train.

ACKNOWLEDGEMENTS

I would have dedicated this book to Comic Boy, but he's already mad enough at me for putting as many of these anecdotes into a book as I did and I'd rather not get murdered in the park next time we go for dinner at the pub. So, Comic Boy. Thanks for not murdering me so far. I appreciate not being dead.

I have to thank so many people. Jess, Cinn, Nikki, Cho, and MJ, to name a few. Thanks for putting up with me rambling about this book and sharing the anecdotes about Comic Boy in the first place.

If you're still reading this at this point and you're not one of the aforementioned people who've had to put up with me while I wrote this, then a huge thank you to you, too. You're the other reason I'm still writing these things.

xoxo

RECOMMENDED READING

Here is (an abridged list of) what Scott and Emma would be reading:

EMMA:

SECRET SIX - Gail Simone, Dale Eaglesham
DAREDEVIL - Mark Waid, various artists, trades
SAGA - Brian K. Vaughan, Fiona Staples
THE WICKED AND THE DIVINE - Jamie McKelvie, Kieron Gillen

SCOTT:

THE VISION – Tom King, Gabriel Hernandez Walta
THE OMEGA MEN – Tom King, Barnaby Bagenda, Jose Marzan Jr.
DARTH VADER – Kieron Gillen, Salvador Larroca
THE AUTUMNLANDS – Kurt Busiek, Benjamin Dewey

ABOUT THE AUTHOR

Kai Kiriyama lives somewhere in Canada under a pile of comics that she probably hasn't read yet, with a looming deadline. When she isn't pretending to read comics, you can usually find her on twitter, avoiding responsibility.

Her website is:
www.theraggedyauthor.com

Made in the USA
Charleston, SC
12 September 2016